embers

AMY KEEN

Fisher King Publishing

Embers

Copyright © Amy Keen 2012

ISBN 978-1-906377-54-0

Cover illustration by Chris Hyder

All events and characters in this publication are fictitious, any resemblance to persons, living or dead, is purely coincidental.

All rights reserved. No part of this publication may be reproduced or distributed in any form or by any means, or stored in a database or retrieval system, without the prior written permission of Fisher King Publishing.

Fisher King Publishing Ltd
The Studio, Arthington Lane
Pool-in-Wharfedale,
LS21 1JZ
England.

Acknowledgements

To my parents; the typewriters paid off!
I am so lucky to have you.

Kris, for 'shining silently' while I
buried my head in this book.

My first ever editor, Simon. Your kind words,
endless enthusiasm and love for these characters
made this book whole. Without you, Embers
would not have come to life and I will be
eternally grateful for every second
you invested in it.

To all the wonderful people in my life that read
the many drafts, conversed with me endlessly on
the topic and put up with my book-related
nonsense; thank you. I can't name you all, but
each one of you played a part in this and for that
I can never fully express my gratitude.

To the good people of Salem and Massachusetts
for letting me borrow some history.

Finally, thank you to Rick for instilling
confidence, helping me make this a complete
story and believing in me. There are not enough
thank you's in the world.

For my boys; Kris and Noah

Witch [noun] a woman, who professes or is supposed to practice magic, especially black magic or the black art most often used malevolently; a sorceress.

PREFACE

I slid the pages into the space below my hands where the air was cold and damp. Grit and dirt gathered under my fingernails as I pushed until I couldn't reach any further. He wasn't far now; the threat of his approaching hatred and ignorance clung to the heavy air and added to my growing sense of claustrophobia. This wasn't just about me, what I could do, it went much deeper. Governed by fear, he groped for answers he wasn't willing to accept and his conclusion was clear - my kind was not to be tolerated.

Somewhere on my bizarre hunt for answers I had lined myself up for capture and my missteps were about to cost me everything. Aware that the events consuming me were about to come to a sinister climax, I did the only thing I could think of. I wrapped myself in my own arms, pulled my knees up to my chin and waited in the dark.

ACCEPTANCE

You couldn't assume popularity. It had to be earned. It took a host of weird and wonderful social rituals to determine a person's popularity and although I had always managed to straddle the complex web that is the teenage poll of acceptance - I was a good student, someone most people didn't seem to mind hanging out with – a new school meant starting from scratch. I couldn't carry anything forward.

"Dammit." Pop Tart goo on my white shirt was a definite no-go for today, potentially the most important day of my life. I had been trying to dress middle of the road. If I made too much effort, the popular girls would automatically hate me and if I didn't make enough, well, I would be socially sidelined and never make any new friends.

I settled on an inconspicuous navy button down shirt,

my dark jeans and my black converse pumps. In Washington I would have felt self-conscious and Brooke – my best friend in the world – would have wasted no time in telling me I looked like I was heading out to do laundry or paint fences. It would never have been allowed. I could picture the scene as she marched me back up to my closet door to reevaluate, 'You look like one of those suspects in a name and shame section of a celebrity magazine.' She was all about celebrity culture and she knew every inch of what it took to pull together the appropriate social camouflage. I laughed at the vision but simultaneously felt the razor sharp stab of fear and loss as I realized that this day – and all the others after – I would have to work it all out for myself. She was there and I was here.

All of that said I knew the look here was; shall we say more relaxed and casual? Despite lacking Brooke's talent for outfit coordination I was more of a make an effort kind of person than not. I just wasn't used to actually having to put it together myself without her to hold my hand and make sure I got it right. Today was important though and I knew I was right to choose blending in over wearing some beads and obsessively fixing my hair. Anything to disappear into the crowd on this day.

I stared at myself in the mirror in the hallway; not yet hung, just precariously propped against the previous owner's questionable paisley wallpaper. A sickening marriage of acid yellow and browns, so many shades of brown. It was just another in a long list of reminders that this wasn't my home. I pushed down the overwhelming urge to throw up; unsure if it was the paper or my gnawing sense of angst about the day ahead.

I had to duck to see myself properly and I felt my knees tremble below my hunched frame. I didn't know why I was so nervous. I had never really struggled making friends, it's just the friends I had – the ones I left behind – were made when I was in kinder garden, so I was a tad rusty. I reminded myself of the time I managed to make a pen pal after one summer train ride to see my grandparents, we wrote to each other for like ten years, so I must be personable enough that this wouldn't be a total disaster.

OK. I didn't look bad. I was never my biggest fan, but I didn't think I was ugly or unfashionable, just OK. Just around the right amount of OK to make a decent impression. I brushed my hair from its sleep induced beehive and some of the fiery red hairs escaped; they littered my shoulders while the rest snaked around the shape of my brush. Shimmying myself free from the debris; I straightened my shirt and gave myself a long stare. You can do this. You made the right choice. This was a great idea.

I heard Mom leave as I stared at myself and pulled my mane into a ponytail. I felt a twinge of anger that she hadn't mentioned anything about today, but to be fair to her, I had begged her not to make a big deal of this, people moved schools all the time, right?

'It's ok to be nervous sweetie, you're bound to feel uneasy, it's natural. But no-one doesn't like you. You'll be out making plans with your new friends before you know it.' She had pep talked me crazy over the weekend. How different could small town Massachusetts be to Washington anyway? I didn't allow myself to answer my own question; instead I picked up my car keys, threw my bag over my shoulder and, with a sigh, stepped into my new life.

The school was really close, in fact, if I had known how close I would have left the car at home, but I was there now and the stress of returning and trying to make it back in time on foot was too much today… so I chipped the car in next to a shiny black soft top - maybe it wasn't so small town here after all. I found myself staring at my distorted reflection into its tinted windows – my hair ablaze with the fall sunlight – wondering who here drove something like that? Somebody whose parents had some kind of major league job round here for sure. I looked beyond it and there were three or four more cars, a reassuring split of the ostentatious and the normal; I didn't stand out with my mom's Japanese hatchback, just blended in. If I was lucky, no one would even notice me.

I rested against the hood, just staring up at the buildings beyond and contemplating the future it held for me. I shoved my cold hands into my jacket and felt my fingers brush against the cool, gloss paper of one of many leaflets I had picked up as part of my Salem education; a curriculum devised by my parents to ensure my happiness in this bizarre place. I pulled it out; it was six sides of slick advertising about what made Salem great and I was surprised by the lack of Halloween reference. Pictures of cool sidewalk cafes, manicured public spaces and absolutely no black cats. The tagline; Still Making History, resonated with me – surely a nod to Salem's non-commercial, candy company past. This town was determined to prove it had more and I was one of the people it would have to work hardest to convince. At least all that was over now, the worst I had to be afraid of was the wrath of a teenage population, who I was presuming would be the same as everywhere else – unaccepting of new kids, determined to weed out and highlight my insecurities, other fun stuff like that. I sighed, stood up straight and headed in.

The school was small, really small to me. Its red brick façade made it look much older that it could have been. Bright, tidy pathways fed into the building from all directions punctuated by flower beds that lay bare waiting for spring. I chose the nearest path and followed the signs to the main office. The corridors were quiet as I had arrived before most of the student population, for which I was amazingly grateful.

The woman behind the desk was probably not much

older than my mom, her hair was short and it made her face look rounder than it was. She was very smiley, which caused the butterflies in my stomach to freeze for a moment.

"You must be Scarlett Roth? We've been expecting you." Of course she had, I practically quadrupled the student body. I prayed I was wrong.

"Yeah. I was told I had to report in this morning?" My subconscious failed to hide how exposed and vulnerable it was feeling as I found myself pulling my arms across my chest and looking down at the industrial grade carpet tiles once electric blue, now fading from the weight of a thousand teenage feet. I almost couldn't hear her words over my internal monologue of horror stories as I prophesised about how many ways I would embarrass myself over the course of the day. I must have heard something as I reached out and took a timetable and a heap of slips from her hand, and I knew I needed to hand one in at each class I went to. Math first, great.

I walked down the corridor that stretched for miles and was met with only a handful of stares. Mostly I was absorbing the silence, occasionally interspersed with the metallic clang of a locker door and the shuffle of books. In my bid to negotiate the room formations I had stopped concentrating. My breathing hitched and my pace was halted as I watched the start of a snowflake-like dance; my paper class slips fluttered furiously to the ground. In the time it took me to roll my eyes at my unbounded clumsiness I dipped my knees to pick them up and the floor was clean and paper-free. My slips were still nestled in my left hand. I had officially lost it. Day one, seeing things – excellent.

I took a few more tentative steps, only half looking where I was going; most of my attentions were focused on composing myself and fighting the urge to turn and run – all the way back to Washington. I bypassed a busy looking swarm of the indigenous population, all gum chewing, hair twiddling popular girls with handbags instead of book bags and vanity boxes where their lockers should be. Most of them dutifully ignored me, I was hardly a threat.

One of them – a slim girl with a barely-there plaid skirt approached, I started to panic but my fears were allayed when she pulled her luminous gum out into a thread on the tip of her manicured index finger. Children did that. She eyed me cautiously as she dramatically flicked her white-blond hair. Apparently real people actually did that, who knew? She stopped just a foot away and sucked the gum back into her mouth with a little pop before looking back to her friends with an obnoxious giggle. This could only be bad. Blond and Shapely proceeded to shoulder bump me so hard I dropped everything in my arms as a cacophony of her clones cackled into their hands. I would have been destroyed with deep, gut-wrenching mortification but the air of weirdness that enveloped me as I watched my class slips tumble to the floor – exactly as I thought I had seen moments before – was a little distracting. Flushed and reluctantly teary, I gathered my things and scurried off like a mouse to where I hoped I would find some more of the people a bit more like me. Without wanting to betray my demographic, I couldn't help but think that teenagers really sucked at times.

I hadn't given any thought what it might be like to be the new kid. In the past I had always felt sorry for the one that turned up in the middle of the semester when all the seats in class were taken. Strange how different it felt to be the one on the receiving end of the inquisitive glances. If anything, it served to remind me that I definitely couldn't hate attention more and another wave of white hot panic flooded through my veins. I was beginning to realize what a crutch Brooke was for me and within moments of stepping inside this alien institution it was clear I was only so middle of the road accepted because of her. I allowed some of my thoughts to escape, the ones I had been suppressing since I left my dad, my life, my friends and my en-suite bathroom behind me last week and was met with the overwhelming desire to cry. A solid, aching lump rose in my throat and I defiantly swallowed it before negotiating the slowly busying corridors.

Maybe it would have been better for me, staying with my dad in Washington. When he and Mom got divorced I wasn't pushed and pulled like those kids you see on talk shows. There was none of me being torn between them or used as some kind of emotional weapon. In fact my parents were a disgrace to divorce; so understanding, willing to compromise and amicable that I was given more choice and freedom than anyone else my age could have expected, but when Mom got the curator's job in Massachusetts it didn't seem right to leave her alone. She would have been fine I am sure, and never had I wanted to believe that more, but I was here now, enrolled and I had promised Dad I would try and look happy about it.

'No-one is making you do anything Scarlett'. His voice had been so firm. I knew he was right, I made this choice and one way or another I would make my time here memorable.

Math wasn't my ideal way to start a new life, but only one more year then I would be free of trig and equations and this place. I chastised myself for the on-going monologue of complaining and self-pity, I had to give this a good shot, it was hardly like I had been shipped off to some archaic outpost, and it was still modern-day America. Really, how bad could it be?

By the time I had done math and chemistry I seemed to have found a couple of acquaintances. It was far too early in the often fickle world of teenage relationships to call them friends, but they were interested in me, as the new girl it seemed everyone was.

Lydia was the first person to actually speak to me.

"You must be Scarlett?" She passed me the workbook Mr.. Gilligan had left for me on the end of the desk and carried right on. "Sorry, I know you must have heard that about a thousand times today, we don't get many new kids, especially two weeks into the semester. People don't really move here." Shocking.

"No it's ok really." I lied. I was happy to be talking though, but not so happy having to pretend that moving here was the best thing that has ever happened to me. She was petite, elfin like with platinum blonde cropped hair that showed off the tiniest hint of mousy brown roots and she possessed a totally enviable figure that suggested she might be a gymnast or dancer. Her eyes skipped about when she spoke like everything she was thinking was so exciting, she couldn't possibly decide what to say next. She had a barrage of questions for me and after finding out we were in history together next and that I didn't know another soul in this torturous place, decided to carry on with the quick fire inquisition. I didn't mind, it was better than feeling like a complete loser.

Two hours down and I think she knew most of my standard personal information, I had little time to get in any questions of my own, but I liked her and I could see us being good friends given a little time. Her mom was a teacher at the junior school and her dad was the owner of a local hardware store, she had a brother who was at college in Boston and a dog that slept on her bed, how that came into it I can't remember. She played with her hair as we talked and she gesticulated constantly which put a smile on my face more than once.

"So is your mom really into the whole witch thing, is that why you ended up here?" She stared right at me, eyes wide like she was waiting for some extreme reaction. I guessed people were in two camps here, she was obviously in the pro-witch history camp.

I knew from the start that my mom taking the job as curator at the Salem Witch Museum would be a talking point. It seemed most people were pro-Salem history and thought the witch stuff was fun, but I didn't want them thinking my mom was some magic obsessed weirdo. I tried to put myself in Lydia's mind as she took a mental tour of our house expecting to find it full of dusty books, with a cauldron where the stove should be. I flashed forward to Halloween, I could have a strong advantage on the party front - unlimited access to the museum goodies would surely make for a good night.

"It's not really about the witches, why she chose here I mean." I kept answering her questions as the bell rang and we headed back into the hallway.

"She's a Historical Archaeologist, specifically American history. She studies historical artifacts and documents." I threw my book bag into my new, inherited locker with a thud and noticed the second hand faded stickers of smiling pumpkins and black cats, people really were into the witch thing here. I continued feeding Lydia with the detail and she continued not to notice how dull it all sounded.

"The museum got a whole load of new items and with the vacancy coming open for curator they called mom in to date and catalogue everything. So here we are." I looked down as another pang of sentimentality for my old life washed over me. Lydia didn't say anything but her expression told me that she had seen my moment of pain. She grinned a huge grin and linked my arm in hers to steer me into the lunch room.

The noise was loud but of indeterminable content, a few hundred voices mingled with the clattering of plates and cutlery. I grabbed a soda to accompany my home-made bagel, which I had to say looked pale and bland next to Lydia's chicken chowder. I hated food envy, I always wanted what the person next to me had and it made choosing meals in restaurants an overly stressful experience. While I was lost in a food fantasy, Lydia was still talking.

"Hello... Earth to Scarlett." She raised her voice to break my daydream and I flicked my eyes back up at her apologetically. "Scarlett, this is Taylor." She signaled towards a willowy blonde girl who was pulling out the seat to the right of me. She was having a baked potato; I would have swapped for that too. I sensed I had left another overly long gap in the conversation as Lydia waved her hand in front of my face and rolled her eyes playfully, I hoped. I couldn't wait for the new girl self-consciousness to pass. It was exhausting being on tenterhooks the entire time.

"She's in some of our other classes; the three of us are going to have so much fun." Lydia was clearly excited and I felt grateful to have such an acceptance already, even if only from one person. Taylor's height and beauty made her look older, and made me feel plain. She could have passed for twenty easily. Her face was pretty, but the way her hands twisted within one another suggested she wasn't overly aware of it.

Taylor asked a few questions, when she could squeeze one in against Lydia's machine gun fire conversation. She was more like me, happy to be social but not keen on attention. When the stereotypical jock walked passed our table and wolf whistled at her she lost her train of thought as her cheeks were flooded with a blush. She was funny in her own way and she dressed like I had wanted to this morning in a simple white vest under a really cute vintage leather jacket and jeans; her long hair twirled into loose curls and she wore just a hint of lip gloss. Maybe I could try a little harder tomorrow without any repercussions.

I enjoyed the rest of our lunch break, the girls introduced me to a few other people in our class, including a couple of guys who were fascinated to hear all about me and Washington, but both of them were clearly either staring at my chest or doing the obligatory marks out of ten for the new girl as they didn't really engage in any genuine conversation.

"What about those guys, nearest the window?" I was getting the hang of paying attention and making a considered effort to be talkative, I didn't want to lose the two friends I had.

"Oh my god... they are the sports freaks. All of them live for Phys Ed, between them they ace every activity the school offers. That guy..." She gestured with her fork to the tallest of them all who was leaning on the window frame, sports drink in hand, naturally.

"He aced the state swim trials, medals and everything. But his Coach caught him chugging back anabolic steroids like jelly beans. Big drama. He was suspended and ordered to take some rehab course. He was a lost cause anyway." She smirked. "A reliable source tells me he isn't all that if you know what I mean?" She added an exaggerated wink before erupting into a mass of giggling hysteria; her dainty hands slapped the table repeatedly as she waited for it to pass. I couldn't help but join in, Taylor was laughing too and it wasn't until a tear ran down my cheek that I realized I meant it; I was having fun.

"So?" She wiped her face and shook her head playfully to rid herself of the giggles. "We can categorically say height and you know what do not go hand in hand. Shame really, he's pretty cute."

Lydia carried on dissecting the lunch room into the social hierarchy. Pointing out table by table who sat where, what the gossip was and whether or not I should waste any of my time in getting to know them. As my eyes moved around the room I was met with more than a couple of inquisitive glances back, just in case I needed reminding I was the new girl.

"And that," Taylor added, nodding towards the final table, which you couldn't help but notice as being the top of the food chain, "Is Jacob Mayer and his friends. He is so dreamy." She dragged out the vowels for effect and already I could see why. He was sitting down so I couldn't tell his height accurately, but he looked tall. He had broad shoulders and angular features.

I allowed myself to glance over, two of the guys on his table were throwing food at each other, it seems male teenage behavior was universally pathetic. The attractive one forked his food around his plate but let out a snigger as a ketchup covered fry slapped his friend in the face. Mr. Mayer's face was quite compelling, kind of attractive in an obvious way.

Pressing the fact that this one was clearly the centre of attention for the female population here Taylor added, "He is super popular but hangs around with the same two guys all the time. That's Tyler to his left and Jason on the right, both football aces and focus of the cheerleader leading squad's attentions. Jake seems to quite like his own company though, so if he were to speak to you, or hang out with you that's like, incredible." She slid her plate away and picked up her bag signalling it was time to go. Tyler and Jason were standard jocks. Broad shoulders, sculpted cheekbones, complete with the swagger that came with intense adoration and unchecked ego.

"It's a total honour if he wants you around him." By you she meant the collective, I could see no reason why the most popular boy in school would want me around him. Although I liked the idea that I might just have what it takes to cut it. Realistically I was resigned to my fate; the last lunch table on the right was not where I belonged. Realism was definitely the key to avoiding soul-crushing disappointment.

Taylor and Lydia weren't in my next class but they dropped me off at the door like concerned parents on the first day of kindergarden and waved me in. I nodded and smiled so as not to appear rude, but I found the whole thing pretty uncomfortable. I didn't want any more reminders that I was new, that I only knew two people in school and that when everyone was talking about their social arrangements in class I was likely to be doing nothing this evening except returning to my strange new home. Mom would definitely be working late to make the best impression. Dinner for one, great.

I chose the better of two empty seats. It was either the back row – which clearly would send the wrong message about my self-interpreted levels of coolness or the one slap bang in the middle. I went middle. I pulled out my special 'I'm the new girl' slip and left it on the edge of the desk. It drew the attention of the person sitting next to me, and he spoke.

"So... you must be the one everyone is talking about?" His eyes locked on me and I felt the blush move up from my neck and pan out across my cheeks. His voice shook my earlier thoughts of ordinary and shot them to pieces, accompanied by that voice his face seemed suddenly spectacular, I tried to remember how to use words as I looked back. Jake Mayer, talking, to me.

I twiddled my pen as I attempted to answer, which backfired as it spun out of my hand and landed in his lap. He smiled as he passed it back and in the split second I took hold of it I was desperately trying to figure out if I could manage a brief hand stroke.

"Yeah, I'm Scarlett." That was seriously all I could manage, too concerned that I may start hyperventilating. I thought, and hoped that I was just flattered as he was the first guy who seemed genuinely interested in me all day, but there was a nagging inside me that signalled a rather concerning feeling, I may be in the first throws of a crush already. Luckily we were just reading passages from Macbeth and I had just finished that in my last semester at my old school, so major lesson attention was not required.

He introduced himself; cue a host of clichéd mental

images. Jake Mayer sounded older than seventeen, more manly, come to think of it the dark shadow that traced his jaw made him look older too, literally edible. Again I wasn't concentrating on the conversation; I really needed to work on that. I managed to answer a couple of questions, minimising the risk of major embarrassment by keeping my responses to a maximum of ten words. Just form the sentences Scarlett. And repeat.

"I heard your mom got the museum job? That's pretty cool. Bet you'll get to see some pretty weird stuff before it goes on show?" He was simultaneously sucking me in while he flicked through his textbook, but oblivious to his power. "It's cool you chose to come and support your mom, I am not sure I could up and leave like you did. High School sucks as it is without having to move to a new one in your last year." Still looking mesmerising he jotted some notes down in the margin of his book. His writing was kind of angular like his face. I was trying to work out how he knew so much about us, but the desire to find out kept being replaced with other, less socially-acceptable-on-a-first-encounter, thoughts and desires.

I found the whole conversation incomprehensibly difficult; coherency had upped and left me, stranded. I answered his questions and re-told the story about my mom and dad's divorce five years ago, concerned the whole time that I was potentially boring him to death, but every time I managed to hold his gaze and not my breath I could see he was listening, taking it all in.

The hour went impossibly fast, despite my silent pleas for it to last forever and I flinched at the stab of disappointment as the bell rang. Then he said it, something I really hadn't expected after a conversation of such obvious pleasantries. But something I was already sure I would remember for the rest of my days if only for the strange, warm eruption of anxiousness and delicious hunger it unlocked. Casually as he stepped up from his seat he ruined me with another look. I was disarmed, entirely.

"Really good talking to you Scarlett." Then pointing at me with his pen, "You shouldn't pull your hair back. It's such an amazing color, like fire or something. Really nice." With that he smiled and headed out of the room every inch the unmistakeable social patriarch. His t-shirt was distractingly tight and it showed the definition of his back muscles as he left. What was I doing? Five minutes and I already found myself behaving like a weirdo. Needless to say I didn't manage to utter a response, my cheeks ended up matching the color of my hair and I felt the bizarre explosion of warmth in my stomach again. My heart pounded loudly in my chest and I exhaled slowly to try to regain some composure.

Outside school as the student body piled out to their social engagements I regaled my new friends with the last hour's 'news' amid gasps of glee and excitement. The air had gotten colder during the day and with every word

Lydia spoke a little bit of her breath lingered, dancing around in the air in front of her.

"This is big Scarlett. You've only been here one day and achieved more than most do in years. I cannot wait to see what happens here." She punched me playfully and let out a girly squeak of joy at the prospect of whatever she thought may happen. I shook my head in disagreement but something inside me stirred and I allowed myself to think, maybe. Probably not, but maybe.

I stared at the car, wishing I had walked so I could take in the route on the way home. Though it pained me to admit it, Massachusetts knew how to work the Fall. It was beautiful, the trees were literally glowing with amber, red and burnt orange and the chill in the air was refreshing, cleansing somehow.

The house was dark, and cold, apparently the heating wouldn't be sorted for another week, some mix up with the boiler, so we were on plug-in heaters and extra blankets. Like camping, Mom had said, never really my thing, but the house looked kind of cute. I bypassed the lights and opted for candles, you couldn't see as many of the unopened boxes that way and it seemed more relaxing to me if I couldn't see all in one go how completely alien this place was to me. I wondered how long the feeling of home took to grow.

After a day of bizarre social interaction, potential boy

infatuation and food envy I rooted round in the fridge. We may not have unpacked but we had prioritised filling the refrigerator. I moved a carton of eggs to spot last night's lasagne hiding at the back. I tossed it in the microwave and let myself get lost in some thoughts until the beep made me jump. I plated up the rest for Mom with a side salad, otherwise she would have eaten something completely devoid of nutrition for the sake of convenience. I left it on top of the stove and blew out the candles before I headed up to my room.

The house was a little Hansel and Gretel-esque. From the road it looked a bit creepy, its dark wooden façade slightly obscured by old trees, but as you came closer it looked warmer somehow with its old fashioned wooden stoop that looked like it was missing one little old lady in a rocking chair. Mom chose it because it reminded her of her grandmother's house, that and it came with forty acres of land along Pudding River. I had to hand it to her, the views were great and it was nice to actually hear nature going about its business. I especially liked the bridge over the river, suppose not many people have that in their backyard. Our house in Washington had the typical suburban lawn, a few well placed tubs and a disused paddle ball table from when I was six. I looked out of the window again and allowed myself to like it, a bit.

My room was as close to home as I could make it. I had the same midnight blue curtains held back with the same over the top tassled tie backs. My pictures were already on the walls, Mom had hung them for me when she arrived two days before me, trying no doubt to ease the pain. It seemed I was a little too much of an open book and she could tell without much digging that I was struggling, but it was only day three, much could change.

I changed into my sweats and pulled on my woolly bed socks, it was freezing. I stared out the window momentarily, trying to get accustomed to my new view which looked, though it pained me to say it, really very beautiful in the twilight. In a bid to placate me for the move, Mom had given me the biggest room. It had dual aspect, so I could see both the drive and street beyond, as well as right across the back, trees in every direction and just a hint of the bridge connecting our yard with the woods.

I pulled the curtains closed in one swift movement then slumped backwards on to my bed. My mind raced, I thought about my friends back home, I even tried to call Brooke but chickened out after one ring. I knew the chances were it would serve only to send me over the edge and some of the tears I had worked so hard to suppress in front of Mom would escape with unstoppable force. So I distracted myself, making a list of homework from today's lessons, hanging up the rest of my clothes that were in danger of living in garbage sacks for eternity and then filled the shelves above the desk in the corner of my room with my books. These were what would probably get me through the really tough times. I had always had an obsession with books, for as long as I could remember. My parents were both big readers and real book purists; in our house you loved books, you treated them well and you appreciated them. I suppose it was in my blood. I stroked the back of The Catcher in the Rye, one of my favourites and considered where to place it. It was faded and curling at the edges and I couldn't help but lift it to my face to inhale the smell of oily printed paper and time passed before giving it pride of place.

I stacked mountains of well-thumbed classics mixed juxtaposed with piles of escapist teen fiction on top of each other and wedged them in with the silver 'S' shaped book ends my dad had given me as a birthday present the year before. I missed him, the void I had been feeding with activity opened up again, growling. No longer distracted, I felt heavy and emotional.

Retreating to my bed I switched to lamplight and read through some of the local pamphlets Mom had brought home. She left them on the key table next to the front door as a hint for me to 'give Salem a shot' and learn some stuff, so I humoured her and had been carrying them around with me for two days. There was nothing to keep my interest, so I rolled onto my side and tucked my hands under my cheek, my legs migrated up till my knees were balled up to my chin. My understanding of the foetal position was that it was a sign of a craving for security, safety, warmth; I would have settled for any of those.

I must have drifted off because no sooner had I been feeling sorry for myself than I was woken by Mom stirring her coffee loudly in the kitchen. I could faintly hear the radio, or perhaps the TV, so I threw off the covers and prepared myself for whatever Salem 'Home of the Spellbinders' High School could throw at me. Although I was quite aware there was only thing I wanted it to throw at me, Jake Mayer. I was being a total loser for even contemplating anything to do with him and I knew it.

Clothes were less of a challenge today, since I had been able to gauge the dress code first hand. I pulled out some black straight jeans and my white vest with the lace hem and wrapped myself in a blue wrap cardigan. I was about to pull my hair up, I had it all scrunched in my hands when I remembered what he said, just the thought sent me a little dizzy like I was having a blood sugar dip and I steadied myself against the door frame. I was losing it. But I still let my hair fall about my face, I ruffled it with my hands pulling some hugely chemical smelling product through it that Brooke had bought me; apparently all the celebrities used it.

Once my eyes stopped watering from the intoxicating effects I glanced at myself, and to give her credit my hair looked a lot more like a team of stylists had stormed in and made me over to look effortlessly effortful. My hair's waves were loose but it curled more as it reached the ends near the center of my back. And psychological or not, it did look shinier, glossy.

Remembering Taylor's minimal but effective make up, I brushed a hint of blush onto my cheeks and blinked twice over the mascara wand before grabbing my bag and following the smell of cinnamon bagels into the kitchen. Without looking up from pouring her juice Mom slid me a plate with a toasted bagel on it and turned the radio down a touch to make for more a more relaxing breakfast time.

"I'm so sorry you had to come home alone sweetie." She eyed me cautiously, expecting me to be angry. A twinge of guilt stabbed me in the gut, had I really been that pouty since we arrived?

"I am working from home today. The new collection is much more extensive than we thought. Some private collector has been harboring some of the most significant artifacts from Salem's history in his attic for years. He has been picking things up from private sales, auctions and other collectors, it's really quite incredible." Her eyes were fuelled with excitement, she sipped her coffee whilst trying to gauge if I was interested enough for her to continue, I must have looked convincing because she did.

"I mean some of this stuff, I don't know where he got it but there are more first-hand accounts of the witch trials in there than I have ever seen. That coupled with artefacts from the witches themselves and what seems to be journals and drawings of the trials." Her mouth full of bagel muffled her words. I think the next word was 'astonishing', something to that effect anyway.

I nodded in all the right places and gathered that she was working through the list of items today and setting up a 'clean zone' in the dining room to examine some of the documents. Which meant I, with all my teenage germs and filth would not be allowed within ten feet of that room until she was done.

"Anyway, so I will be home when you get in today. That's what I was getting at. How was school? Did you make any friends? Are there any cute boys? Did you join any clubs or societies?" She asked me about as many questions and did so at such a similar pace I couldn't help but think of my new friend and her same technique of information gathering.

"School is…well just school I guess. It's small and I have covered a lot of the subject matter at ho…in Washington but I made some friends. And no I didn't join any clubs Mom, it's been one day, I am eighteen years old and therefore trying to avoid actions that may constitute social suicide at such a sensitive time."

The corners of my mouth lifted into a smile and she smiled back. I went on to tell her about how giddy Lydia was and how Taylor looked twenty and the boys seemed to love her. I skirted round the boy question embarrassed by the fact I had allowed one in particular to enter my thoughts on several occasions since my close encounter of the inconsequential kind in English the day before. I certainly didn't tell her that's why my hair looked like I was doing a shoot with InStyle today.

"That is great honey." She paused and her face went really serious, like she was in pain. "Look, I want you to know I really appreciate what you have done," she corrected herself, "are doing for me." I started to speak but before the words could leave my mouth she placed one finger over my lips like you did with kids. "Let me finish. I know this is hard for you, and that you miss your father and your friends, but I want you to know if at any time you want to go, you can, no strings. I won't stop you. I am just grateful that you were willing to try." She rubbed her hand across my shoulder and looked at me, really at me and I knew I had done the right thing. She needed me, even if she didn't say so. I moved round the table and threw my arms around her neck, she smelled so good, and I realized that smell had the power to make me feel at home, so maybe it was all OK. We had always been close but this move was the most tangible way I could show her how much I loved her, and needed her in my life.

We didn't linger after that, we did the dishes. No dishwasher here. She kissed my head and headed off into the dining room to begin the transformation.

I pulled my stuff together, book bag, phys ed kit, yuk, and then grabbed my car keys before remembering how short a drive it was and putting them back down. No, no driving; I needed to familiarise myself with my new neighbourhood. So I set off on foot.

The route to school was straightforward and lined with houses of all shapes and sizes. I liked that, the mis-match nature of everything made it fun to look. I saw some of my new neighbours arguing through their porch window and dipped my head forward so that my hair would cover my face and I wouldn't be exposed for the nosy parker I was. I also saw some kids I recognised from school joining the sidewalk a few hundred yards ahead, they must have spotted me because one of them turned round quickly to get a look before returning to the conversation.

I felt less nervous now I knew at the very least I had Lydia and Taylor to talk to or to talk at me and that was a reassurance. They were waiting for me at the main entrance, I had seen them from a distance laughing and comparing shoes, they seemed genuinely excited to see me.

We were early so sat in the almost deserted lunch room chatting, with only a few stragglers hanging around. There was a tall gangly boy I recognised from my English class sat alone on the next table, the drum beat emanating from his iPod was like a heartbeat in the background. The girls asked me more questions; I dutifully answered them all and perfected half listening half observation. It worked out especially well when the side door to the cafeteria opened and in walked Jacob with two of his food throwing friends. He made them look like such little boys, towering above them in height and physical presence. His general demeanour was mature, sexy.

My mouth may have been open a little, not so attractive, but it didn't stop him speaking, to me, least I think it was to me. I forgot to start listening I was so absorbed in taking in every detail of him. His brown hair tousled upwards, another wonderfully tight t-shirt, grey this time and from the front I could see that his chest and stomach were very likely to live up to my god-like expectations. It was entirely possible that below that veil of cotton was a body to match Michelangelo's David. An accidental and audible sigh of appreciation left my lips and I dipped my eyes in embarrassment.

"Ah, I see you took my advice. Looks good." He strode passed me looking back to flash me a brief but undisputedly spectacular smile, his teeth were also perfect. I looked at my hands which were wringing themselves stupid and it took me a minute to realize the background noise had gone, Lydia and Taylor were silent. I glanced upwards to find their faces frozen in what could only be described as utter disbelief, shock, or maybe horror, the unbreaking silence made it hard to tell. Meanwhile the door shifted to a close slowly and the scent of him flooded my nostrils. It was probably just normal cologne but to me it seemed like a combination of sweetness and hormones. My eyes were fighting against my decision to look at the table,

I allowed myself a cautious glance at him, and was gratefully for my eyes' disobedience.

I attempted to re-boot the conversation. "Sorry, what were you saying about classes, who do I have with what?" Nothing, not a word. They were catatonic. Then suddenly, in perfect harmony they broke their silence with serious volume.

"OH MY GOD! Oh my god." Lydia was jigging around on her seat like a lunatic and Taylor was shifting her hand palm facing up from me over to the vending machines where Jake and his friends were loitering somewhat like Danny Zuko and the T-birds in Grease. Her mouth a gaping 'O' the whole time.

"OK. So he talks to you. He actually talks to you in class, which he never does and now he talks to you again, completely unprompted with an audience?" I knew it was meant as a question but I was sure I didn't know the answer.

"This is huge. He must like you. The cheerleaders are going to die, literally. I mean they will hate you. HATE you. It's brilliant." I wasn't entirely sure how a hoard of angry girls vying for my blood at my new school could be a brilliant thing. I was not in the market for making enemies right now. I had visions of them turning up at my house in the middle of the night, torches lit like in the witch hunt, with a special hate filled cheer just for me, great.

"It's no big deal. He spoke to me, so what?" That was a question and I did know the answer. The answer was that by some unbelievable twist of fate I had at the very least caught his attention and whether or not I could maintain it seemed inconsequential at this moment. I was high as a kite, but I knew I must not show it. The girls would find it all too easy to swap their excitement for jealousy and I did not want that at all.

A few more minutes dissecting the very brief 'incident' were spent before the bell's drone dragged the lingering student bodies up out of the cafeteria and on to class like extras in a movie about the undead. All except me; I was walking on air. I felt high, as if I had been doing some kind of drug, not that I knew what that was like. I was just tingly and pleasantly lightheaded as I glided through the crowds without noticing the 'new girl' stares and comments. I found myself smiling.

The lightness passed and shifted to burning curiosity, what sports did he do to get so buff? What car did he drive? Did he live on my street? God I hoped so. Would he speak to me again or was that it? One fleeting moment or would there be more? Could there me more? I really, really hoped so. That would make life here in Salem more than bearable.

Gift

The rest of my first week went largely without incident. Jake spoke to me a little in English on the Friday, asking more questions about my reasons for moving, what music I liked. Between my shallow breaths which I desperately tried to hide from his hypnotic eyes, I managed to deliver a few coherent answers. His breath was cool and pleasant when he turned and spoke close to me. Though the publicness of the early morning cafeteria 'conversation' was never repeated, he seemed willing to talk to me in close proximity, maybe he was embarrassed to be seen with me, with my probably obvious flushed cheeks and faltering eye contact.

The student body – Lydia and Taylor included – was raving about the Halloween ball. My God. I couldn't think of a worse occasion. It was obviously not until the end of October, it was only September 20th, but apparently six weeks was simply no time at all to find the perfect dress or date. I like to plan an outfit, but not even I got this ahead. I assumed any Halloween occasion here was an all-out affair, fear for what lay ahead consumed me and I played with my food rather than face the barrage of questions I knew was coming.

"I want Tyler to ask me to go with him, but every time we speak he talks to me about everything other than the ball." It was the first time I had seen Lydia not looking excited about something. She shook her head, ridding herself of the self-pity I knew she hated and then her eyes fixed on me. I couldn't escape.

"Before you ask me no I haven't decided to go, therefore haven't picked a dress and will definitely not be asking Jake Mayer to take me." I held her gaze and kept my face serious, I wasn't trying to be rude but a social event on this scale was not my idea of fun so early on in my new life, it was just too much. And I felt a twang of chagrin as I realized I did kind of want to go, if I were being honest, but only with him. Get real.

When I opened my eyes on Saturday morning my room was dark under the weight of my curtains, as I pulled them apart sunlight streamed into my room and the woods beyond looked warm and seriously inviting. I hadn't made any plans; it seemed bizarre to use up my first weekend sitting around talking dresses with the girls so I had made my excuses. Mom needed my help, boxes to unpack etc. They seemed fine with it and I promised to join in more next week.

Mom had been locked up in the dining room all week so I was surprised to find her at the table when I went down; she winked at me and brushed her hand across my cheek as I passed to get to the juice. We exchanged stories about the week and she invited me to go with her to the museum and have a sneak peak at the new additions.

"Sounds good to me." And I surprised myself, because it kind of did. I had read everything on my bookshelf twenty times so some documents of major historical significance really might be interesting.

We drove to the museum, it was another short drive, probably unnecessary but there was a real chill in the air and it helped me get my bearings. Plus it was nice to spend some time with Mom, it gave me an opportunity to show her I was interested and most importantly happy, or at least I could be. We pulled off Washington Square to park, a cruel coincidence that it should be called that. My excitement for the day ahead waned slightly at the stab of sadness for my real home as I looked up at the imposing building.

It was not what I had expected; though I don't know what I thought would be suitable. In Washington the museums I loved were crisp, contemporary looking places. This was something else. The building was a tall and weeks was simply no time at all to find the perfect dress or date. I like to plan an outfit, but not even I got this ahead. I assumed any Halloween occasion here was an all-out affair, fear for what lay ahead consumed me and I played with my food rather than face the barrage of questions I knew was coming.

"I want Tyler to ask me to go with him, but every time we speak he talks to me about everything other than the ball." It was the first time I had seen Lydia not looking excited about something. She shook her head, ridding herself of the self-pity I knew she hated and then her eyes fixed on me. I couldn't escape.

"Before you ask me no I haven't decided to go, therefore haven't picked a dress and will definitely not be asking Jake Mayer to take me." I held her gaze and kept my face serious, I wasn't trying to be rude but a social event on this scale was not my idea of fun so early on in my new life, it was just too much. And I felt a twang of chagrin as I realized I did kind of want to go, if I were being honest, but only with him. Get real.

When I opened my eyes on Saturday morning my room was dark under the weight of my curtains, as I pulled them apart sunlight streamed into my room and the woods beyond looked warm and seriously inviting. I hadn't made any plans; it seemed bizarre to use up my first weekend sitting around talking dresses with the girls so I had made my excuses. Mom needed my help, boxes to unpack etc. They seemed fine with it and I promised to join in more next week.

Mom had been locked up in the dining room all week so I was surprised to find her at the table when I went down; she winked at me and brushed her hand across my cheek as I passed to get to the juice. We exchanged stories about the week and she invited me to go with her to the museum and have a sneak peak at the new additions.

"Sounds good to me." And I surprised myself, because it kind of did. I had read everything on my bookshelf twenty times so some documents of major historical significance really might be interesting.

We drove to the museum, it was another short drive, probably unnecessary but there was a real chill in the air and it helped me get my bearings. Plus it was nice to spend some time with Mom, it gave me an opportunity to show her I was interested and most importantly happy, or at least I could be. We pulled off Washington Square to park, a cruel coincidence that it should be called that. My excitement for the day ahead waned slightly at the stab of sadness for my real home as I looked up at the imposing building.

It was not what I had expected; though I don't know what I thought would be suitable. In Washington the museums I loved were crisp, contemporary looking places. This was something else. The building was a tall and deeply unsettling dark bricked church. An actual church. Its large wooden doors dominated the front elevation and its name was painted in gold lettering above the door beneath a huge stained glass window, it felt like some kind of gateway to the past. It made me a little uncomfortable and a sense of acknowledgement for the history behind it chilled me. Those were such dark, strange times and I felt it somehow incongruous that we and thousands of others should recognize it through a series of sinister plastic mannequin reenactments. I'd done my research and knew what to expect but it still felt weird knowing I was about to see it for real.

"Isn't this great Scarlett? Have you ever seen something so cool?" I offered an awkward half smile as I followed Mom inside the door; which was already propped open, and I observed the throngs of tourists as they wandered round gawping at the exhibits, their audio tour guides emitting muffled sounds into the air. Some had expensive cameras hung round their necks, hands clasped to either side ready in case something supernatural happened and they could capture it.

Mom's office was small, but really smart. It was right at the back of the museum, out of bounds to the prying eyes of schools kids and holiday makers. There were unmarked boxes piled up in the corner and several piles of photos which looked like they were the ones she must have been working on as I recognized the pattern of our dining room rug in the corner of one of them. Her deep mahogany desk was vast. It had an inset of worn red leather and I could faintly smell it in the air, combined with paper and polish. You could tell by the slightly worn patches on the carpet at the foot of the desk that this office was well-used and I felt a little swell of pride for Mom as I watched her slide into the equally grand chair and push her glasses up the bridge of her nose.

I flicked through a bunch of papers balanced precariously on the corner of her desk while she logged on to her computer. They were photocopies, grainy and quite hard to focus on.

"What are these?" I was starting to get interested as a few words jumped out at me, 'hunt', 'witch', 'persecution', 'fear'. I never shied away from the supernatural, I found anything with a hint of the other worldly about it feverishly exciting so I couldn't help but pick them up. My maternal grandmother used to always fill my head with fairy stories and tales of the mysterious and I suppose they stuck with me. My mom was always telling her off and rolling her eyes; frightened I would be scared and have nightmares, but it was quite the contrary. It was those stories that sparked my love affair with books; something about the triumph of good over evil and magical things we couldn't always understand was addictive. Looking around this room, full of unread pages, I felt comfortable and like myself.

"That's some of the journal pages we found in the new collection, we are having the pages mounted and encased this week, they are going to be unveiled Halloween week in a new exhibition." She was distracted by something on the screen, so it was really the right time to ask the question.

"Could I maybe read the copies? I won't show anyone or anything?" I looked up, she was biting her lip, she always did that when she was concentrating and it was one of the many traits I inherited from her.

"Mom?" I pressed. My words broke her concentration, her lips relaxed and she looked at me over the top of her glasses.

"Ok. But seriously, do not…." she paused for dramatic effect, but I could tell from her face that she wasn't kidding. I could potentially get her into a lot of trouble if I didn't pay attention. "Show anyone, or tell anyone. If this gets leaked it could put the whole exhibition in jeopardy. These diaries are really exciting, we learn a great deal about some of the more obscure and secretive people in Salem at that time, things that have not been seen for hundreds of years. So, if you can do that then sure."

I was convinced this was another bid to placate me following the move, but I cared little for the motivation behind it, it was a nice, albeit chilly day and I had some exciting new reading material. This made for some good times.

I sloped off not long after as it was clear Mom was going to spend her entire Saturday with her head in front of the computer, so I took the car and headed back via town. Maybe a little history could be fun. I parked up and admired the tree-lined streets beyond and the way even some of the stores had white-picket fence style frontages. I answered the siren call that came from the first bookstore I found; naturally this was on Washington Street, ouch. I bought a book on the witch trials and it was immediately obvious the woman serving me thought I was a tourist because she tried to sell me every piece of witch related crap she had, and her collection was pretty vast. I hadn't given Salem the credit, well any credit at all really, that it deserved, there were heaps of cool little shops punctuated with eateries, it wasn't the desolate hell hole I had previously thought. I was definitely warming, but wasn't willing to fully admit it.

I dropped my purchase back in the car I escaped the Washington street name maze and found a grocery store, heavy reading meant lots of snacks. I had already planned to go out and sit near the bridge across the yard, I liked the river, it was peaceful and right now the idea of sitting on its banks was pleasing, and in that moment, while I thought that I felt like I was home.

Snacks carefully selected I tucked the bag under my arm and wandered for a while. Absorbing every detail of this new place. I headed down Lafayette Street and stumbled across a hardware store; fairly sure this was the one Lydia's family owned. A man wearing an apron that matched the logo on the grey clapboard fronting was tidying goods in display racks outside the front door and though I couldn't be sure, something about the curve of his nose reminded me of her; it must be her dad. He was busy with stacking small boxes and leaning brooms against the doorframe. I couldn't help but smirk at the notion of modern day witches existing here of all places and casually popping down to Lydia's family store to collect their replacement.

I found myself paused on the opposite sidewalk just staring at the shop with its old-fashioned, painted signage; it had a comforting, simple charm and I was smiling at the idea of one day knowing all this fully, the people and their lives. Green's. I said the word out loud; I hadn't even bothered to ask her last name and I felt a pang of shame. I was so caught up in feeling sorry for myself about being the new girl that I hadn't even thought about it. I made a note to be more interested and apparently less self-involved when Monday came around.

It felt nice to see into her family a little, some of the backstory. I had all of that at home, with Brooke; I practically lived in her house since I was ten. I would get cards from her family at Christmas and little gifts for my birthday. I missed that stability that came from history and I longed for it. Seeing Lydia's dad there I wanted to run over and introduce myself, start to create the same here. I had to stow my hands in my pockets to avoid waving at him like I knew him.

I breathed in deeply, feeling the cold air as it made its way into my lungs and looked up at the clear, azure sky. A pleasant, light breeze carried the scent of pine and fall into my consciousness. I looped back on myself and saw another imposing building, something more like a town hall, majestic in height with beautiful red bricks and green doors, it was charming. The City Council had banners outside advertising a craft day running to support the upkeep of this and several other historical buildings.

I wasn't going to go in, I was eager to get back to my plot by the river and start a mammoth readathon, I had already altered my course to cross the road and head back to my car when I heard a familiar voice.

I spun round to be met with the sight of him. His eyes were dark, tired looking today, but he still looked perfect. His rust colored, woolen scarf masked the bottom of his face a little and the obscurity frustrated me; I was hungry to see the whole thing. I don't know how but I opened my mouth, and to my shock and relief real words, aligned in real sentences came out. A higher power had granted me the gift of speech.

"Hi… how are you?" I didn't care about the answer, not in a callous way, just whatever it was he looked amazing and staring at him, stood here in the cold was surprisingly enjoyable. He looked at my hair briefly, down again, he clocked it I am sure and then I allowed myself to relax into the intonation of his voice.

"I'm good." He paused and pulled a hand through his hair; I thought and hoped it carried a hint at him being nervous. "So, are you heading in to check out the local wares?" He sniggered, clearly expecting that I would be, and I was not sure if I should be insulted. I reorganized the bag in my hand, bringing it over my chest in order to make myself less fell a little less vulnerable.

"No. I mean I am sure they are great but I have stuff to do at home. What about you?" As the words left my mouth my inner monologue cheerfully chipped in with a 'does he look like he is into crafts to you?' Then to my surprise he said yes.

"Don't get me wrong, it's not through choice. My dad heads up the Resident's Committee, I always get roped in to lugging boxes and setting up tables at events like these." He looked embarrassed; I could have sworn I saw a flush of pink enter his cheeks. This had to be a good sign.

"Why don't you come in, I can introduce you to some people?" Shooting me a furtive glance he gestured forward encouraging me to join him. I moved towards him stumbling slightly and reached out to steady myself, only to find my hand rested against his chest. He looked down at me and smiled again, I was getting good at this whole playful, hopefully endearing fool thing.

"I can see you need looking after anyways so you might as well come with me for a bit." He was laughing now he put his hand on the small of my back and gently pushed me forward. I was a wreck; my body was in a full scale revolt against me, legs trembling, cheeks blushing and hands shaking so much I had to tuck them into my pockets to avoid being caught out. My inner monologue was hysterical with laughter at my inability to be a normal human and all the while my back buzzed from his touch.

Once inside Jake toured each table with me introducing me as the new girl, when he did it I somehow didn't mind so much. In fact, I was fairly confident that even if he introduced me as the Bumbling Idiot City Girl, which would be fair comment based on his experiences of me to date, I wouldn't have cared.

It was mainly Salem's older female contingent in attendance. Each one of them knew him by name and lit up when he spoke to them. If they been a few years younger I could have sworn they were flirting with him; there was a definite pattern of face fanning and eyelash fluttering, it was embarrassing. Their attentions shifted though when the doors opened and the air from outside travelled through the room, bringing with it the scent of leaves. It was the man that followed they were interested in; they seemed to all slightly adjust themselves, like they were standing to attention. This person held court here, but their body language was open, warm. They respected him.

The figure in question was a tall man with short grey hair, thinning on top. He stepped into the hall and approached us confidently in his expensive suit with a powerful stride. Like with the guy at the hardware store, there was that faint familiarity and a furtive glance to Jake, whose frame had stiffened slightly at the side of me, confirmed that I was probably right to assume this was Mr. Mayer Senior. Also Chief of the town's Resident Committee, voice of the people and well-loved local doctor, that bit I gleaned from a stolen snippet of conversation amidst the craft community. He was big news apparently.

His cologne hit me forcefully, attacking my senses. It was a strong, musky smell that oozed money and power. His face met mine as he thrust a large hand toward me.

"Well then let me guess. You must be Angela Roth's daughter, Scarlett?" His face was not dissimilar to Jake's, very angular and distinguished with age, but he lacked the warmth I recognized.

"Yes sir." I extended my own hand which thankfully had fallen back in line and shook his with a firm grip. Ouch; he squeezed hard and kept unwavering eye contact the whole time; ensuring that those few seconds felt like hours.

"Jake here mentioned you two had been in some classes together." My stomach erupted into a mass of huge somersaults; he had been talking about me. I glanced at

Jake who was focused on his father, but I thought, hoped I could see a little bit of tension in his face. Tension was good, it meant it was true and Jake rolled his eyes in my periphery and I smiled.

The amusement faded fast as without warning, normality was consumed by something all the more concerning. The room started to spin and my legs felt like they might buckle while my stomach leapt as I watched in horror as the events unfolded before me. One of the women we had been speaking with minutes before was crossing the hall's wooden floor, carrying a tray of glasses for refreshments. I watched as her ankle twisted below her and she lurched forward, hurling glasses and a huge jug towards the floor. The objects smashed with a loud echoing crash, shards of glass splintered in every direction, as she fell she tried to steady herself but an irreversible course was in motion. She fell to the floor and my stomach heaved as I saw her reach out for her right wrist. A large angry looking shard of glass was protruding from it. She wailed in pain and her face contorted with the agony as blood ran down her arm and moved in a sinister puddle across the floor beside her. So much blood. I literally felt the color drain from my cheeks and the searing burn of the shock ripped through me, weakening me further.

Jake's eyes were wide with genuine fear. "Scarlett, are you ok?" I couldn't work out what was happening, but as soon as his voice registered and I blinked I could see that the spot on the floor where moments ago there had been carnage, was gone, floorboards clean and debris free. I was reminded of the weird moment on my first day when I had been so sure my class slips were scattered everywhere, but there was nothing. I was unsettled and frightened and if it weren't for the vanity surrounding my chance to interact with Jake I may have lost it all together.

Aware that something seriously weird had just happened I scanned the room and saw the woman in question stood, casually chatting with one of the others. She was fine. My head was still spinning; I couldn't make sense of what I had seen, or thought I had seen.

"Urm, yeah, sorry. I felt a little weird there for a moment." I forced a short unconvincing smile to the both of them. I don't think I was fooling anyone, they both stood transfixed on my face. I stuffed my hands back in my pockets as soon as I realized the shakes were back, though the trigger this time wasn't nearly as welcome as the last.

"You ok, do you need me to get you anything? Do you want me to call your mom?" Jake was genuinely worried, which had I been in a better frame of mind would have delighted me. His voice was soothing now; calmer and even in my current state his hand on my arm was still warm and exciting.

I shook my head and looked up to meet the gaze of his father, who hadn't said a word yet. His face was pale, motionless and I could have sworn he was angry, but I didn't understand why. He fixed his stare on me and refused to look away. I held for a moment but felt increasingly intimidated by his expression and I couldn't shake the very real sense that he didn't like me, not at all. I didn't understand what had just happened, but I don't think it could have evoked that reaction; he had only just met me.

Jake glared at his father. "Dad, what are you staring at? She probably just needs to eat something." He escorted me out holding me gently by the elbows and force fed me one of the Reeses cups I had in my bag of goodies. As we left the hall I could feel Jake's father's eyes boring into the back of my skull, I spun round to check and there he was frozen to the spot, glowering.

It took me a good twenty minutes to convince Jake I was ok to drive. I thought it was easier to go along with the blood sugar issues than opt for the truth which was that I had seen a horrible accident that didn't really happen, which in no uncertain terms meant I was insane. By the way please take me to the Halloween dance? No, honesty was definitely not the best policy.

I left him there in town and saw him standing watching me leave in the rear view mirror, the pleasure of that chipped away at the black space inside me filled with fear about what I had seen, or not seen. The drive home was a bizarre mix of emotions, elation as I recalled the two occasions today when he touched me. The feel of his skin even against my clothes made something inside me stir and fizz. Then in horrific contrast my mind would switch to the images of the blood, the woman's twisted face and the helplessness I felt as I had watched paralyzed. What was that? I had nothing. Not a clue.

I dropped my bag of snacks on the table, grabbing a couple and took the copied pages of the journal out with me into the yard. The sun was still shining but the breeze took the edge off any potential warmth, I had to zip my coat up and pad the ground with a blanket from the garage to get comfortable. I needed this, some time out and to try and relax again. I had been making so much progress before the afternoon's events. I focused on a series of deep, revitalizing breaths.

I started to flick through the pages; the first few of which looked like transcripts. The language was interspersed with officious jargon. I tossed them back into the folder, pulling out a huge stack of pages that were covered in handwriting, bound together; here must have been two maybe three hundred pages and it weighed a ton.

I was just about to make a start when vibrations from my cell broke my train of thought; I fought through my layers to find it, I immediately wished I hadn't.

"Sweetie, where are you? Dr. Mayer called me, he says you were with him earlier and you looked sick?" My mom was wonderful and she cared, but usually a little too much. This would take weeks to blow over, there would be temperature checks probably daily, and if I didn't manage to convince her of my perfect health, there was potential for letters to school telling them to keep an eye on me. It struck me how trying to sound calm and well when recalling a psychotic episode was tough.

"Mom, I am fine. What did he say? Calm down." I swallowed the returning panic and focused on the task in hand; playing down one of the most bizarre and frankly terrifying experiences of my life.

"He said you just froze and went pale and looked like you were going to throw up. He said you were like that for a couple of minutes, they didn't know what to do with you." She was talking so fast my head was spinning trying to process it. Hearing her talk about it drilled the reality into my mind; I was scared and whatever had happened was not normal.

"Look, I hadn't eaten any lunch; I just got a little light headed. I am fine honestly." I lied, well, this time. "No, don't come home, I am just sitting, reading. I ate something and now I feel great, never better."

Ten minutes of lying seemed to do the trick; she finally agreed to stay at work. The black space flexed in my gut, I felt my lungs tighten so I lay back for a second, letting the cool air blow over my face. The breeze defeated the dark and I got back into the manuscript from the museum.

Word after word I just got hungrier, I was turning the pages so fast I had to force myself to slow down so I didn't miss a syllable. Life, love, loss, it was all in there. My mystery heroine wrote candidly about the boy she was seeing in secret, how she would sneak out under cover of darkness to sit with him. There was even an account where she described word for word the evening he told her he loved her. I shifted my weight as after so many hours my legs were starting to tingle. I had to stand to shake off the threat of cramp. I took my chance to re-fuel and hoped if I ate something it would ward off another episode; though I knew full well that it had nothing to do with my blood sugar. I returned from the kitchen with a soda and some of the chips I bought; the sight of my little picnic and bookathon was pleasing. Simple things.

It wasn't long before I was absorbed again. Their relationship was a traditional star crossed lover's tale. His family higher up the social hierarchy made the social implications of any union between them catastrophic. So they made do with sitting, being near each other, feeding off the warmth of each other's skin by proximity alone, it seemed nothing 'impure' as she put it was ever discussed, though it was insinuated that the thoughts had crossed her mind. I felt a synergy with her at one point in particular. A shared longing or excitement.

This night was of all the nights by far the most significant. We sat behind the church, a bizarre place for the Deacon's son to run to, but he reassured me we would not be sought out here. The moon was bright; we sat in silence for a while, merely looking at each other. His eyes magnificent, he met mine and brushed a smooth, welcome hand over my face before tracing the line of my lips with his finger. His hand on the small of my back made me feel improper, but I did not shy away, I leaned closer and allowed myself to feel his breath on my skin, sweet and warm. I didn't allow him to kiss me, I couldn't bear it, having to know what that was like then stop. But I dreamt of him that night and every night since. I love him.

The pain in my legs had intensified and it was only the distraction of my discomfort that alerted me. It was almost dark. I shuffled the document back into my bag and followed the glow of our porch lights back to the house.

Mom was home within seconds and I thanked my legs for driving me inside before she walked in, that would not have helped my case. Ill and missing would have tipped her over the edge.

We ate together, I more enthusiastically than I felt in the mood for, just making sure there were no holes in my façade. The reading had made for amazing escapism and I replayed her words in my head every time the darkness inside me made me scared about my potentially faltering mental health. By the time we were done and I had finished working on Mom's relaxation I sloped off to bed, my feet heavy and the dull ache of concern throbbed in my stomach. I tried to read but not even the power of history's lovers could convince my eyelids to stay open.

I dreamed of the scene again, the one where I saw what I saw, but this time it was from above. I watched as my face turned porcelain white, when she fell, then while she bled, and I saw Jake, his fear and his concern. How he had touched me. The feelings were still real, his warmth radiating through my clothes. But it changed, the scene unfolded differently. Jake's father grabbed my arm, with his face in the same angry twisted expression and then he spoke, but the buzzing of adrenalin drowned out his words. He was looking at me, meeting my gaze from above the scene; he knew I was watching him. I strained desperately trying to hear, my eyes fixed on his lips. It looked like he said 'I know'. I was none the wiser; I don't know what he thought he knew? Everything faded to black and I had to resign myself to the fact I wouldn't find out, but as much to the knowledge that his reaction to me was also, unusual.

Sunday passed without incident, I had chores to do, a week on and the house looked no more lived in, a bystander would have struggled to determine if we were moving in or moving out. So I committed myself to sorting a stack of boxes in the hall and moved them to their rightful homes, carefully arranging memories of our past life in Washington on shelves and in cupboards. I managed about an hour before I was so bored I found myself picking things out of and then putting them right back in.

Mom was having a rare day off, raking the first results of fall from the yard and re-staining the bridge while the rain held off. I stood in the kitchen for a minute watching her, wondering what she was thinking, she looked happy, calm and rested; I wished I could say the same for me. Last night's nightmare had made for restless sleep and although it wasn't even noon, I felt weary. Refusing to waste the day I grabbed the manuscript from its resting place next to my bed, threw on a sweater before pulling my hair back, not without the image of Jake's disapproval in my mind, I smiled at the thought of him and headed out to where Mom was working.

She didn't lift her eyes from the brush strokes as she spoke; she was biting her lip again. "Hey sweetie. What you doing out here?" Her face crinkled as she watched a drop of wood stain land on her boot. "Dammit." She attempted in vain to wipe it clean; instead she managed to smear the drop into an inch long stain. I could feel the inevitability of the corners of my mouth turning upwards; I had to suppress a smirk by pulling the neck of my sweater over my chin. She knew I would be laughing, she knew everything about me; at least she did until yesterday.

When she went to speak again she tried to look annoyed, but instead she was overcome with a little hysteria and laughed until she cried. I liked watching her laugh, tiny laughter lines, something which I inherited from her, forked out from the corners of her eyes which were bright with amusement and the stillness that came with seeing me a little more at ease.

"I thought I may camp out here this afternoon if the weather holds and read those notes you gave me." I slung a blanket down on the ground in the same spot as I had the day before, put my back against a tree and slid down into my position for the day. She nodded, her face focusing back on the brush and she hummed to herself.

It wasn't long before I was back, engrossed in my love story. My heroine was still battling to see her love, sneaking out in the middle of the night. I enjoyed reading about her siblings, the quarrels and chores in the house; it was weird how little had changed.

I read on and on, absorbing every nuance of her life. Her words were witty, and filled with excitement, trepidation and real emotion. I related to her, I pictured myself in her shoes sneaking out to meet Jake, with the clear, although confusing disapproval of his father in place of the Deacon.

I found myself shifting locations, inadvertently exploring the garden as I uprooted my reading spot and swapped it round to ward off the stiffness that threatened to send me back into the house and away from my story. I didn't stop reading until Mom called me for dinner, it was dusk again and it wasn't until I stood up that I realized how long I had been there, my butt was fast asleep and very unforgiving of my choice to sit on the cold ground for hours.

We ate fajitas sizzling from a pan; it was Mom's

specialty, though I don't know how much resemblance it bore to the real Mexican version. I ate three before slouching into my chair defeated. I made my excuses and headed upstairs by seven, I knew I had some unanswered emails from Dad and Brooke to attend to and I wanted to cram in some more reading before bed. Just the thought of the word bed woke the slumbering weirdness I had been feeling, since yesterday, but I handled it, focusing on everything else.

Hey S

How's it going in witchville? Mom says you've been sick, are you better? What was it?

Mom must have been worried to get Dad in on it. I knew they probably thought I was deeply psychologically traumatized by the move, and although it seemed like a reasonable conclusion to jump to after yesterday I couldn't help feeling it had nothing to do with that.

So, how is school? Did you make new friends? I know Brooke is missing you, she called by to pick up a couple of her CD's, you should call her.

OK, sorry for the inquisition, email me back, SOON! Love Dad xx

I typed back frantically trying to answer each question fully; he would take any omission as a sign of a problem. One down, one to go. I messaged Brooke, filling her in on Lydia and Taylor, careful not to over hype them; I didn't want it to sound like I had replaced her. Then I hinted that there may be a boy, teasing a couple of facts about Jake in because I knew she would bite. Job well done. I picked out clothes for tomorrow, grabbed a shower then settled by lamplight to another night of reading; followed by what I hoped would be a more peaceful night's sleep.

It was getting better, a line had been crossed, and there was a kiss. I could not get enough of anonymous author, the description was perfect, I feared I may have drifted into some kind of fantasy land as I distinctly tried, pretty damn hard, to imagine me and Jake taking their places. I also took a moment to silently acknowledge how creepy it was for me to imagine these things in quite so much detail; I had only just met the guy.

His hands moved up from his sides where they had been clenched, knuckles pressed up against his skin and he brushed the back of his hand across my cheek. It was cool, refreshing and I felt the same warmth within me rise. My heart was beating so fast I could barely catch my breath. He leaned towards me, eyes fixed on me, holding my hands with his now, he brushed his lips against mine, slowly, before pressing them onto me with passion. I tried to resist but I was rendered completely powerless.

I couldn't take any more for one night, at least maybe now I had some good dream material for Jake. Confident that he was likely to now think I was a freak and never speak to me again, I would have to make do with dreaming of the moments I had forfeited through my odd behavior. I was perplexed at how much the thought of him not speaking to me wrenched me, I couldn't think about that now. I definitely didn't want to rely on his attention as my only source of happiness here; it was wrong, and certainly very unhealthy.

Taylor was waiting alone when I arrived at school the next day. The lot was quiet; I reminded myself I could probably take a good extra half hour in bed and still be on time in future. We discussed the weekend; I purposely skipped over the events of Saturday afternoon. She was excited about the dance and had been provisional dress shopping with her mom.

"Seriously, it's probably the most beautiful dress you've ever seen. I am going back next weekend to try it on again. This gives me just under one week to convince my mom to buy it for me." She rubbed her hands together like a cartoon baddie and grinned. I lost the thread of the conversation then as the black car I had clocked on my first day glided into the same spot. The windows were tinted so dark I couldn't see who was inside. As the door swung open I pushed up on my tip toes for a better view, Taylor was not at all interested. I guessed she already knew the answer. I felt that familiar chagrin as I realized how eager and pathetic I looked. She kept talking in the background, but I heard nothing.

It made perfect sense, why I didn't put it together

before is beyond me. Jake Mayer stepped out throwing a fleeting and very casual glance in my direction, but no smile, no wave. I was hurt but not surprised, he didn't owe me anything. The best I could hope for was that he didn't tell everyone else what a huge freak I was. I had English later, so maybe I could beg for his silence in exchange for not embarrassing him with too much conversation in future. Of all the people to reveal my latent weirdness to in a new town; it had to be the beautiful, popular one, naturally.

I fumbled my way through gym; avoiding contact for fear that my lack of concentration would result in some poor bystander being sent to the nurse. I could only think about English, and it wasn't Macbeth that was bothering me.

His seat was empty when I arrived, I didn't know if that helped or not, would it have been less weird if he was already there? I fanned my books out to occupy myself and one of Jake's food throwing crowd had switched to paper and was hurling them at the guy in front, but a poor aim meant several landed in my lap. I considered throwing a glare his way to signal my displeasure but thought better of it.

Having maintained the head down position I didn't notice Jake walk into class. I felt him before I saw him. The atmosphere on my left side changed as soon as he sat down, the air cooler and that familiar smell. I didn't remember how to move, I risked a fleeting glance. He was staring right at me. Waiting for me to look up.

His voice was calming, cool and every word considered. "So, you ok?" I breathed a sigh of relief, speech was good and he didn't seem angry or upset so the car lot must have just been one of those things. I pulled my hair behind my eyes to remove the veil and looked back at him. He was so beautiful, I don't think I'd ever met a beautiful boy before, cute yes, but not like him, he was magnificent. I remembered the first day, in the lunchroom and I had he was nice but something clicked with the first sentence he uttered and now, well I was basically powerless.

"Yeah. I felt fine right after I told you." I insisted a little too much, my tone sounded harsh and when the words reached his ears he looked put out by them.

He paused, flicked through a few textbook pages then exhaled deeply. "What really happened Scarlett?" He looked right into my eyes, the intensity made me look away. I am pretty sure I looked as confused as I felt.

I rested my chin on my hands, "What do you mean?" I was nervous to find out where this conversation might go.

"When you got sick, you were looking, really looking at something, but there was nothing there." He thought I was insane, I knew this would happen, I felt a wave of hot embarrassment flood over me, impossible to conceal.

"Wh..what are you asking me Jake?" I really wanted

to know, I didn't like the tension that had developed in his voice and the atmosphere between us.

"After you left I went back inside, my dad was stood in the same place and it all seemed fine, but maybe twenty seconds later Mrs. Caulfield, the nice lady who we met, with the green sweater...." his voice trailed off, I could see him thinking, almost hear it, trying to piece it together before he said something that sounded insane. I was hot not because of his angular face and the way his lips moved, but because somehow he knew something weird had happened and I was worried that what he was about to say was only going to make it weirder. I was terrified, not about what he was thinking anymore but about what this meant for me.

"She fell right by where we had been standing; she tripped carrying this huge tray and hurt herself pretty badly. We took her to the hospital, she needed forty stitches Scarlett." For a second I reveled in the sound of my name leaving his mouth, his voice made my name sound prettier, but any pleasure was short lived as I registered what he was saying, he sounded like he was blaming me and my defenses sprang up.

"That's awful." I stopped myself from continuing, there was no way I was giving anything away, I could have gotten the wrong end of the stick.

"You knew it was going to happen didn't you?" He glared at me, a mix of confusion, fear, pity in his eyes. I looked down, forcing a mocking laugh.

"What? Jake, that's insane." My smile dropped. His hand was on mine, below table level so the rest of the class didn't feel inclined to stare. He stroked the back of my hand with his thumb, it felt amazing, having his skin on mine without the barrier of clothing was more incredible than I could have fantasized.

"Look. Scarlett, I don't understand what happened but you saw something, I know you did." He was still stroking my hand, which made it difficult to focus as the ripples of tantalizing pleasure from that small gesture moved up my arm. My breathing had shallowed again.

"Ok, say for arguments sake that I did see something? That I didn't get sick. What then? You going to tell the whole school I'm insane, that I see things?" I was snapping, aggressive to mask my overwhelming feeling of vulnerability.

"Scarlett, I'm not judging or threatening to tell anyone anything. When I realized what I thought had happened I just wanted to see if you were ok. I was worried you know." A flicker of happiness twitched inside me. He was worried about me.

He looked right at me, still. "Does it happen often?" He was genuine, caring and now more attractive than ever. My own god-like knight in shining armour. At least if I was mad he didn't seem to care.

"No. That was the first time." I was aware now of several pairs of eyes upon us, eager, wondering what was possibly interesting enough about me to draw the attention of this amazing person. I was with them, I had no clue.

"Anything since?" He definitely believed me, which eased my discomfort.

"Nothing, at all, it disappeared as quickly as it arrived." I was calmer, openly insane in the company of the object of my heart's desire, but not so tense. It felt good to have talked about it.

The corners of his mouth curled upwards, breaking his serious expression for the first time, his eyes softened and a wide smile broke out on his brilliant face. Mimicking him without intent I smiled back. "What's so funny?"

"I've never met anyone who could see the future before. It's kinda cool." That's when I realized his hand was still on mine. I couldn't hide my excitement; my face was giving me away. "I wonder if you'll get to see good stuff too, instead of just drama and gore." I hoped he was thinking of the same potentially positive implications of seeing the future, our future. I reminded myself not to be ridiculous.

"Me too. Though if I am honest I wouldn't mind never seeing anything like that again good or bad, it's totally creepy." I hoped it was a one off, but the idea of seeing my future with Jake wasn't all together bad.

"Least they don't hunt witches anymore…you'd be screwed!" He laughed again and I smiled back, I really would be.

Macbeth completely neglected; student population suitably intrigued and a decision with my new confidant that no-one else needed to know. I felt better than ever, not only had he touched me, but he still wanted to speak to me and see me at lunch. This would be interesting, I doubted Lydia's ability to remain conscious when the excitement of that revelation hit. I was nearly right, she hadn't passed out, but she went a funny color like she might explode.

"He's waiting for you. He's sat on his own and he keeps looking over here." She was twinkling again, the way she had when we first met, I really liked that about her. Taylor was not so giddy, she was feeling neglected I think, all the more reason for me to go.

I went to pull out the chair and he beat me to it, pulling it back and gesturing for me to sit down. Another smile, this one better than the ones I had seen so far, though I seemed to think that every time.

We traded crappy stories, talked about music, apparently our tastes crossed over a little. I took this as another sign of our inevitability to end up blissfully happy. I didn't share that particular thought. We laughed in unison as we realized between his friends and Lydia and Taylor we were the center of attention. Cautionary glances from his camp and excited if not a little over the top thumbs up from mine.

He sped by me on the way home, accelerating loudly as he went; I could have sworn I saw a smile to accompany the sound of his horn. We had discussed the ride home at lunch, I assured him I could manage the walk, but really I couldn't face the barrage of questions from Mom, too early for that. The feeling of my time with him stayed with me, warming me from inside, arming me against the cold until I reached the house.

PARALLEL

The house was warm when I got home; the boiler had finally been fixed. I celebrated by changing into a vest and my sweats and grabbing a snack. I was annoyed at myself for not remembering everything more clearly, that always happened to me; the more excited I got about something the harder I found it to memorize. My visual memory ended up being sketchy, black dots clouding all the best bits, his eyes, the exact way my hand tingled when he touched it. Though I had enough to be going on with.

I heard Mom get home, the door latched softly behind her. She obviously thought I was asleep, and I was too giddy to go and have the 'how was your day conversation', my elation was almost tangible like electricity, she would have clocked something.

I buried myself in my reading, trying to be a normal human, one that wasn't a twisted fortune teller or boy obsessed weirdo. I had even toyed with calling him; I looked his number up after I met him in town. It was sat right on my desk, doodled on with hearts and swirls, taunting me. I was becoming more of a loser every second I spent near him, though his willing acceptance of my madness did bode well for any other faults I may have, but widened the gap between us. He was perfect and hugely popular, I was, not.

The house's new found warmth was a little overpowering I propped my window open to keep me cool and awake while I took in my daily dose of my mystery heroine's life. My head was throbbing and my ears were buzzing; a deep, low hum reverberated within me and it dizzied my vision. I steadied myself back onto the bed and no sooner had it arrived than it was gone and my head was clear. Odd.

I grabbed the book, the pages of which were starting to look tattered, well loved; my partial fingerprints marked the pages I had already devoured. My eyes hungrily marched across the pages and the words filtered in to my consciousness like an alarm bell ringing.

I froze with disbelief; I couldn't believe what I was reading. The words dizzied me, rippling across the page as my head struggled to compute her notes. Suddenly cold again I slammed the window shut and retreated to my duvet for comfort and safety.

It's been three weeks since I last wrote. He has not returned since it happened. I tried so hard to keep it from him, to avoid shackling him with my chains, but the more time we spent together the greater the risk got. I was no match for temptation, his scent, his touch were too much for me. Then when it happened I could see the fear in his eyes, the judgement. I was with him, it was evening time and I saw it. A new vision, a dark and loathsome one. It showed me a horrible death, with pain and fear. I had hoped I would be able to conceal my 'gift', it wasn't always so bad, I had even been able to help people before, when the visions had been good and pure. Had I known my proximity would put him at risk I would not have succumbed. But as the vision took hold my hand was within his, our beings intertwined and somehow it passed from me to him.

She repeated; 'He did not return'. I couldn't believe that was possible, though through her description I was sure the experience she described was the exact same thing that happened to me. And if that was true would I be dragging other people in if it happened again? If I was set to have more of this, the last thing I wanted was to drag others into it, others like Mom, Jake, Lydia. Everyone I cared about would be at risk of exposure to this weird nightmare world. I shut the manuscript, frightened now that the more I read the more I may find out.

I tucked my knees up into my stomach, rolling on to

my side I felt the darkness that had been absent for an entire day start to gnaw at my insides, growing, taking power from my fearful, shallow breaths. There was nothing to panic about, it had only happened once and no one was touching me, so it wasn't exactly the same. I didn't even convince myself.

Sleep was terrible, restless. I had a million shattered dreams, none of them clear but I recognised Jake's face, his horror as he pulled away from me, from what I had shown him. That was a much as I could remember, I wanted just to put it behind me, focus on the facts. It was one time. I am ok now. There is little to suggest I am in the same situation as a complete stranger from the 1600's, the whole thing was ridiculous. My imagination was running wild and I had to rein it in before I drove myself insane.

Over the next few days I spent more and more of my time with Jake, though I tried to save lunch for the girls, it was dangerous to abandon your friends for a guy especially new friends and for a guy that may or may not like you.

English was undoubtedly my favorite subject, I knew why though and I protested to Lydia that it has always been my strongest blah, blah, blah, she didn't buy it.

"I have to say it. I am super disappointed with your sharing Scarlett." She pointed a playful finger at me and jabbed me in the ribs. I knew where she was going but it would be more fun to let it play out naturally.

I stuffed some fries into my mouth to ensure I was

otherwise engaged when she spat it out. I avoided eye contact too, opting instead for spinning a quarter on the table.

"Seriously, I am going mad here. You have some mystery encounter with the hottest guy in school and from that day he waits for you every day like he cannot wait to see you, he moves away from his friends to get privacy and offers you a ride home like every day. What the hell?" She was faking a disapproving look. Taylor, who had been uncharacteristically quiet all week, seemed to come alive when she realized I was going to speak. I think now my attention had been deflected off Lydia a little she felt more comfortable.

"Yeah Scarlett, this is most unusual. We have never seen him interested in any girl. The cheerleading squad practically dance past him every day in gym shorts to get his attention, and he only seems to want you," she smiled, perhaps to hide the fact she, like me didn't understand what he was doing paying me any attention.

Lydia sat patiently, hopeful that the two prong attack would lead to greater spillage. Taylor pressed the matter, her eyes wide. "If you go out with Jake Mayer you will literally alter the social rules of this school. Anything would be possible." It cut me, I wasn't sure if it was meant to but it did. I looked back down at my quarter.

Realizing how she had sounded she backtracked. "Sca... I didn't mean that he was better, I just..." She looked awkward; she didn't know how to recover. I put a reassuring hand on her arm.

"Don't you think I am as weirded out by this turn of events as you?"

Lydia grew tired of waiting; she tapped her nails on the table and rolled her eyes with a loud, dramatic sigh. "Well...we can skirt round it all day, but you haven't actually told us anything." She was getting testy. I liked how much interest this was raising, it made it feel even more exciting and if I were honest it boosted my ego a little.

"There is nothing to tell." Lie. "We just bumped into each other in town, he introduced me to a few people and then I spoke to him in class a couple of times." The rest they didn't need to know yet, if ever. "We just get along, you know. We have stuff in common I guess." I signaled the end in the revelations by sliding my tray away and sliding my bag on to my shoulder. Lydia's thirst was satiated, for now, but she would be back. I really hoped I would have more to tell her. Embarrassed by the kinds of thoughts that ran through my mind I looked away in case somehow they could tell.

When English finally couldn't cheat time anymore I walked to class slowly, measured steps. I would hate for him to see me practically jogging to my seat so desperate to be next to him. I thought of the manuscript, what I had read and felt physical pain at the idea of putting him through anything weird or disturbing like I had seen. I had to be careful around him, just in case.

He wasn't there, my heart sank a little. It struck me I hadn't seen him all day, which was unusual. Mrs. Bodwell was subbing today; she handed out some lame question and answer paper on Macbeth. She left one in Jake's place as she passed. Where was he?

He didn't arrive. I felt so dejected. Maybe this was a signal I was meant to interpret, that I shouldn't get used to having him around. I hated how much I cared where he was. I wanted more than anything just to know he was ok, not sick or in trouble. The fact that he could no doubt look after himself was irrelevant, if he was sick I wanted to be the one to take care of him, the way a girlfriend would. A word with myself was required; I had to stop living this bizarre fantasy out in my mind. He hadn't actually done anything to suggest he felt nearly the same way I did. Hard to imagine him struggling not to pick up the phone and call me, impossible in fact.

I watched my breath forming ghostly whorls as it left my mouth, it was colder today, and I didn't have any fresh memories to pull up from English to heat my walk home. The dark empty space was hungry, desperately willing me to panic. I couldn't decide if I was just worried about him or, if as I suspected with shame, I was put out that he would just not show at all, not concerned with how that might make me feel. He unwittingly turned me into a quivering, hormonal and apparently selfish mess.

Mystery of absence unsolved I ploughed myself into my homework, another evening alone with only my weird taunting fears and my unending thoughts of Jake Mayer - joy. By eight thirty it was pitch black, I tossed the plate from my supper into the sink, which could definitely wait until morning. I poked around my new home, it still felt pretty alien despite being full of things I remembered well, things I knew and that held my memories. For the first time in about a week I wanted to go home, back to Washington, to my dad and my suburban lawn, anywhere but here. I had a tendency to be emotional, I accepted it but it wasn't welcome now. The feeling was so strong it caused a huge throbbing lump to rise in my throat as I climbed the stairs. By the time I reached my room large salty tears had etched a watery map of mascara down my cheeks and I couldn't stop the noise that left my mouth, powerful sobs wracked my body and I buried my head in my pillows to drown out the sound. It somehow made it louder. I was mid-composing myself again when the phone rang, grateful now for the handset in my room I wiped my eyes on my sleeves and cleared my throat, if Mom called she would know, like she always did that I had been crying.

I practiced a quick hello aloud to make sure my voice was up to normality. "Hello?" I did good, quite normal. There was silence for a second and a barely audible but definite intake of breath. Whoever it was had to think before they could speak.

"Scarlett?" It was my turn for a sharp intake of breath now. Surely not? I didn't speak for what felt like an age but my body took over.

"Who is that?" I played dumb in case I couldn't take the disappointment if I was wrong. My right hand was trembling, I picked at a thread to distract myself, winding the length of it round my finger till it went blue.

"It's, urm me, Jake" So he doesn't show up for school but he calls me at nine pm, go figure. I wasn't in the slightest bit concerned of his motives, his soothing voice rushed through me, clearing out all sense of anxiety in an instant. He was like therapy, much needed and very enjoyable therapy. Bottling his effect would make me millions, but I wouldn't share how he made me feel, not for all the money in the world and that really scared me.

"Ahh... hi. To what do I owe this honor?" My tone was playful, mocking and I sensed a smile, but he hid it well.

"I felt bad, about today." He was serious now and silent for a good while, whatever he was thinking needed careful wording obviously. I waited, not offering any steer to the conversation, it was imperative I didn't lead him in any direction if I wanted to hear the truth.

He continued, quietly. If I had been there I think he would have been blushing. "I ditched, I do that sometimes, just to clear my head, you know." I sensed there was more so I maintained my silence. I lay back, propping the phone against my ear leaving my hands free to twirl my hair and pull it down from its ponytail, for him I thought.

"I just felt like, well how I would have felt if I had turned up in English today and you weren't there without any explanation?" He stopped, fearing he had gone too far I sensed it was my time to engage in the conversation. I was glad for the distance, although a strange thing to want it was the only way I could avoid the embarrassment of him seeing the huge, ridiculous grin on my face. Composure, I pleaded with myself.

"What do you mean Jake?" Still smiling I urged for him to give me more, to hear his voice say something I could commit in fantastic audio perfection into my memory. The darkness in my stomach had been spectacularly overturned and replaced with hoards of butterflies that made me feel warm and kind of faint. Grateful for being horizontal I could wait without fear of losing footing.

"Are you making me say this? Really?" He was definitely smiling now and openly I heard it in his voice and I followed his lead. I bit my lip to subdue my giggling stupidity and covered my eyes with my hand.

He didn't wait for me to speak again. "Ok. But don't expect me to repeat this, I feel like such a loser." He laughed, another intake of breath, I could have sworn I heard his heart beating, but if that were true he would certainly have heard mine. My heart was trying to break free from my chest.

Finally he made it to the important bit. "Jesus Scarlett. I like you. I really like you. And I called because I realized if you hadn't been at school I would have been worried and would have wanted you to call me, to know you were OK." A sigh escaped his perfect lips; though I couldn't see him I could imagine them. In my head I traced the shape of his jaw with my fingers and brushed over his lips, I had to stop that, it was too much to imagine that kind of proximity.

"Happy now?" He sounded mad, but I knew he wasn't. I waited a moment, pausing for dramatic effect, enjoying the fact that I had the upper hand just for a moment.

I couldn't do it to him anymore. "Jake. I." Then not for effect, I was stuttering, I couldn't get any more words out.

"If I have just made a complete tool out of myself please let me know, quickly." Insistent and feeling understandably vulnerable he pressed me for more of a response. I was still in shock about what was happening. It seemed more likely to have been one of my fantasies than something that was actually happening to me.

"No. No you haven't. Oh my god, not at all. I'm sorry I wasn't being rude I just can't believe this is happening." There was silence on the line, which I suppose I deserved.

"I am really glad you called, and even more glad you

feel that way." My voice was smiling with me. With the awkward bit out of the way we talked comfortably until gone eleven. My mom had come home around ten, I suitably lowered my voice and turned the light off so she wouldn't find me out, but mainly because I couldn't risk any interruptions, if I was dreaming, I wasn't ready to wake up. I'd allowed my breathing to return to normal once her bedroom door latched shut behind her.

We finally hung up having agreed he would drive me to school tomorrow, I knew it was safe; my mom would be long gone by then. I pulled the duvet over my head and hit my fists against my mattress in sheer excitement. My mouth was dry from all the talking, I reached for my glass of water, but in the dark I knocked the discarded manuscript onto the floor. It fell with a thud and in my haze I didn't even bother to pick it up; I just rolled over and smiled myself to sleep.

I heard the car roll up the driveway before I saw it, gleaming in the fall sun, the black BMW glided over the approach before pulling up right outside the door. He stepped out and propped himself against the driver side, arms folded; looking so inviting I could hardly stand. I pulled on my coat, pausing at the front door to breathe, I needed all the oxygen I could store, I knew once I got within one foot of him I may inadvertently hold my breath.

It really was too short a drive, and today more than ever I wished I had walked, we had walked. We had lost so many valuable minutes by opting for the car. Within seconds we were in the school parking lot. I reached a nervous hand down to unbuckle my belt, colliding with his as he did the same. We glanced at each other, both wracked with anxiety about the contact, the first since we had confessed to liking each other; touching now had entirely different connotations. The spot where his hand touched mine burned with longing, I wanted more of that, more of him. Cool it, I warned myself not to give him any reason to realize he could do so much better than me.

He was at my door in a second, opening it for me. He flashed me a smile; I couldn't stop looking at him. I reminded myself to take in every element of his perfect face, just in case it was over too soon. I was never famed for my optimism but this situation was without doubt the most bizarre and unlikely I had ever found myself in.

We hadn't discussed it but I assumed we would not suddenly be the prom king and queen, running round attached at the hip. I was still looking; some would have classed it as staring.

"I need to go meet Lydia, I, I'm really sorry, I promised her." I looked down fearful that I was making faux pas number one.

He stared back, pensive, thoughtful for a moment. "Relax. I don't want you to change a thing." He brushed his index finger down the side of my face, my eyes closed involuntarily, relaxing into his touch. "I'll walk you there."

He reached down and pulled his fingers through mine spreading the burning from where he had touched me in the car right up my hand and into my arm. He started walking; I lingered for a moment, in awe and relied on autopilot to get my legs moving.

We walked through the same side door to the cafeteria that he always used. The room littered with the other early students, people from my classes and some freshmen conversing nervously about a report they had due. Then my eyes fixed on Lydia. We were about ten foot away, she was distracted, iPod in, books out on the table, no sign of Taylor, one at a time was probably best.

He stopped just shy of where Lydia was sitting, still looking down at her books. He brought my hand up to his face and pressed his lips against my skin before releasing it. I almost passed out but was distracted by Lydia's face that she had broken away from her reading material and I guessed from her face had done so in time to witness Jake's lips on my skin.

He watched my reaction to his contact. "See you in class." Then, back turned he convened with his friends, none of whom I knew, but who seemingly knew more about me judging by the shared glances, across the room.

I sat down, wearing my best poker face. I was doubtful I could hold it, especially taking in Lydia's expression, a tangled mixture of shock, disbelief, excitement and possibly a hint of jealousy. She stared at me, her voice choked by her memory of recent events. It was about two whole minutes before she spoke.

"What the hell just happened?" Her face had softened into an eager and inquisitive expression; she was wriggling round on her chair expectant and longing for info. I enjoyed dragging out the suspense and I made her wait while I pulled a juice box from my bag and popped the foil with my straw.

Her eyes were burning a hole in my head. She couldn't wait any longer; she shoved my arm and rolled her eyes disapprovingly.

I took her gaze finally. "What? Nothing's really happened yet, just watch this space." I shot her a glimpse of my excitement, pretty sure it was all over my face.

She was not satisfied with that analysis. "Nothing's really happened?" She repeated my words with a sharp tone. "So… are you two a couple? What the hell Scarlett, how could I have possibly missed this?" At that moment Taylor arrived and we switched from question and answer to Lydia re-telling in unbelievable detail the occurrences of the last ten minutes. Taylor mimicked her shock and awe and I could hardly hear myself think amidst their shrill voices. They weren't going to let this lie, but I didn't really know what to tell them, I hoped I was his girlfriend but I couldn't assume. I did know that since last night I was happy here, and could be for as long as I had Jake in my life.

I hadn't been able to duck the questions for long; I spent every possible moment in the company of my two crazy new friends telling them every single syllable of my conversation from the night before. There was screaming, giggling and tension as I recalled how Mom had come home in the middle of Jake's confession to me.

As he approached me again my stomach churned and jumped around. I placed a hand on my stomach, pleading for normal behavior. As he got to me he reached for my hand and presented me with another cool, lingering kiss on the back of my hand. The burning returned and fuzzed a familiar line of fire up my arm and the back of my neck. I closed my eyes again, opening them to find him staring at me, smiling.

He continued to stare at me. "I love that." A simple, beautiful sentence that sent a new rush of adrenaline running through my veins. When I was with him most things were possible for me. I was like the superhero version of myself, happiness being my main, if not slightly annoying power.

The next few days were a haze of dreamy moments with Jake punctuated by a series of shrill and excitable conversations with Lydia and Taylor. I avoided my mom like the plague in case she caught the scent of my infatuation and subjected me to an inquisition, still fearful that Jake would come to his senses. I wanted to keep it as quiet as possible, just in case.

"I'm taking you, no more fobbing me off." Mom pointed a finger at me as she projected her best authoritative voice, I didn't have the heart to tell her she was the least threatening person I had ever met. She folded washing in front of herself, mockingly throwing the clothes into a pile as angrily as she could manage, it was a poor effort. I reached out and pulled the clothes away, refolding the ones which had unraveled in her mock tantrum.

"I seriously don't need a new one mom." I lied, I did. What self-respecting teenage girl wouldn't need a new dress for her first social occasion at a new school and with a potential, although yet undetermined new boyfriend in tow? But I felt a twinge of guilt when I thought about how much money she had put into moving. The house had been more than she wanted to pay and although she never mentioned it, I am pretty sure she wasn't getting as much money as she had hoped for the job.

But she was resolute, she wasn't taking no for an answer. So we packed up for a day of mother daughter bonding. We had been used to doing something like this every weekend at home in Washington, but her new job meant I hadn't seen her for more than about two whole days since we moved and I could see it pained her, the guilt. Such a stereotypical mom, in the best possible sense, she was born to nurture, protect and care. Any time she felt she had let that slip she was so hard on herself it was painful to watch. She tossed her keys up in the air in celebration of my concession and winked as me as she ducked her head into the car.

Although shopping would have once been the only thing on the 'What Makes Me Happiest' list, it had dropped several places since I moved. The combination of a more casual teenage population and the fact that I had some kind of sickly happiness on tap from Jake meant I was a little out of practice.

She pulled out the one dress I was hoping she wouldn't, for someone who knew me so well she very occasionally got it so wrong. "This is gorgeous; you would look great in this." Her eyes flashed with excitement and she thrust the dress at me. It was cerise pink, knee length with wide satin straps, it was seriously hideous and had social suicide written all over it, though Mom clearly couldn't see it.

"Mom, I love you. But..." My tone had come out a little more patronizing than I had hoped. She glanced back at me as she submitted and shoved the aberration back into its hiding place, "Good." I concluded, pleased with the diversion.

I pulled the next selection over my head. It was a cream satin halter with black lace trimming the straps which followed the cut into a deep 'v' down my back. I looked over my shoulder at my reflection and tugged my hair band to watch my hair tumble beyond my shoulders. I timidly pulled back the curtain and peered round to look for Mom.

I heard her before I saw her, my view obscured by another row of glittering gowns and occasion wear, the kind moms wear to weddings.

"Oh Scarlett, that is just, wow." She raised a hand and covered her mouth, I thought I saw a hint of glassiness in her eyes, this was a good sign.

"You have to have that one, and some shoes to match. Seriously." She looked around, already seeking the matching accessories, rifling through a basket of beads and bracelets, handing me fistfuls to try on. I convinced her less was more and we settled on just one necklace, a short pearl row punctuated by little black beads, it was perfect.

We ate lunch, talked about how work and school were going; cramming the last few weeks of catch up into the time it took to eat a wrap. It was really nice, it reminded me of our old life, but I wasn't sad, I think I was even happier. Something had clicked and I was starting to feel like I belonged.

The car ride home was equally chatty, maybe overly so. She really loved the chosen dress, she wouldn't stop talking about it, and I sensed all this talk was leading somewhere, but I could not have predicted where.

"You looked so gorgeous in it. He will be blown away." A smile spread across her face and she maintained a forward gaze, waiting for my response. I had to sit on my left hand; it would have definitely given me away, fiddling with a loose curl as I thought about my answer. Turned out the thinking time was wasted I could manage little of worth.

"What? Who will be blown away?" She wasn't buying it.

"Jake Mayer." And with that she turned the radio up signaling she didn't expect any more information, because she already had it. From somewhere.

SECOND SIGHT

I smoothed my hands over the dress, brushing away imaginary creases; I just wanted everything to be perfect. The thought of him standing in my hallway made my legs tremble. I rested a hand on the doorway and took a deep breath to reduce my chances of passing out at the sight of him in a suit.

One last glance in the bathroom mirror, dress, check, necklace, check, little bit although not too obvious makeup, check, and hair perfectly coiffed but down obviously, check. I hadn't anything else to do but survive the stairs. Seemed like more of a challenge than picking the dress or getting ready in only five hours.

I started at his feet, my eyes scanning every inch of him until I found his face, which, if even possible was made more handsome by the contrast of his olive skin against his crisp white shirt and black, perfect suit.

His eyes widened when he saw me, but his face was expressionless, blank, it didn't feel good, not exactly what I had been hoping for. He reached out a hand and escorted me down the last step onto the hallway's wooden floor, my heels making that feminine sound I had missed since moving here.

"Wow, you look sensational. Seriously. Wow." His mouth now hung open a little and I could see his eyes devouring every inch of me, if only. My stomach lept and my heartbeat raced, so much I bet he could have seen the movement through the satin.

I smiled back. He was still staring, "Here." He gestured for my wrist and fixed on a Halloween themed corsage, sadly that was the deal, you didn't have to dress up but you had to have something that represented Halloween. So a beautiful white rose was neighbored by a small faux pumpkin and a black cat. He let out a smirk at the contrast between my outfit and my new accessory.

Much to Mom's upset she had to work so wasn't there for the official meeting, though I knew it was only a matter of time before she pinned me down and made me commit to bringing Jake over. It seemed her information was from his dad, apparently he had taken quite an interest in me since my 'illness' a few weeks back.

He would be at the dance, several of the residents' committee were also governors at the school, so they were acting as regulators to check we didn't all end up drunk on cheap booze bought by an older sibling or making out in the bathrooms. I had to admit, the thought of seeing him again took the edge off my dizzy, delirious happiness. There was something about him, the way he looked at me that day, the thought of his face, his eyes glaring at me from a distance that made me shudder. I shoved those thoughts to the back of my mind and allowed Jake's hand on mine to warm me in that familiar way all the way to the dance.

Lost in his touch on my skin I hadn't noticed the change of course and that we weren't heading to school. I looked around, it was dark but I recognized the Old Town Hall, great, a wonderful reminder of a day I would have liked to forget. "Hey, I thought the dance would be at school?" I questioned, he sensed the concern in my voice.

"No, it said so on the posters, they always have them off campus." He brushed his fingers over my hand again. "Look, I know you probably haven't been back here since you had the, well since you felt ill, but there is nothing to worry about. I will be with you the whole time."

I submitted, helpless against his voice and eyes. "I will be fine. Just stay with me ok?" I pulled his hand towards me and gripped it tighter. "I'm not going anywhere." I was nervous enough about tonight without this on my shoulders. What was bothering me most was that it had been a few weeks of tentative hand holding, lots of late night calls and flirting but tonight was definitely the night for the first major kiss. Unsaid but agreed. He was acting like the perfect gentleman; I wish I could profess to be such a lady. I knew it would be tonight, though I didn't fancy an audience, I hoped we could be alone, at least for a while.

The hall looked entirely different from how I remembered it, the wooden paneling completely obscured by streamers in black and orange. Plastic cats were positioned around the room and piles of intricately carved pumpkins marked the front of the stage where a set of decks were being operated by one of the sophomore's. The music was loud and most people seemed to be there already, which was good because it meant few people looked up when we walked in. Our 'going public' was still cause for whispering, staring and general teenage point and snigger tactics. I didn't blame them, he was seriously out of my league, but I wanted to try for one evening to at least look like I belonged with him.

"Here." He passed me a drink in an orange plastic cup, I felt like I was at a kids' birthday party. We looked at each other and smiled; he held my gaze and raised a hand to stroke my face. I closed my eyes for a second and felt his hand move down onto the small of my back, it fitted there perfectly, and I felt safe and comfortable.

We danced and talked for a good two hours, his hands moving from mine to my back and occasionally my face, which always drew attention. I hadn't seen his father yet, no big worry there.

He read my mind. "My dad is coming soon, he landed the job as one of the bouncers." And sure enough, no sooner had he mentioned him than Mr. Mayer strode into the hall flanked on either side by two men, it looked like something much more ominous than a school dance the way they arrived. Jake waved and his dad acknowledged, but luckily he didn't come over. He shot me a smile but I wasn't buying it, his whole expression was weighted with contradiction, as if his expression was the exact opposite of what he was thinking. I wished I knew.

"You wanna go soon?" He had a glint in his eye and I liked it. I looked back at him and grabbed his hand, I squeezed it and he knew I had answered. We took a seat next to a couple from our English class at the edge of the room. The DJ faded out the chart music and faded in the traditional slow dance number. The hormone level in the hall jumped about one hundred per cent as eyes eagerly, fearfully, requested their partner's hands and led them to the dance floor. Jake put his hand on the small of my back again, the burning warmth returned and we instinctively got up at the same time and found our space on the crowded floor.

"I've had an amazing ti…" I was about to gush how wonderful it had felt being on his arm tonight, how every time he looked at me I wanted to pull him into me and kiss him, how every time he touched me it left a warm, tingling patch on my skin. But that didn't happen, I watched his face twist from eager to frightened as he watched me, his hands dropping to his sides, my legs felt like they were buckling beneath me again but I was still stood upright. My vision went blurry, patches of dark eerie shadow crept into my line of sight. It was happening again. A red car, an old beaten up Ford rattled down a road, it was pitch black, only the headlights and the light of the moon punctuated the infinite black of the tarmac. I couldn't make it all out, I couldn't see the faces of the two people in the front seats, the guy was driving and the passenger was female. Their faces were blank spaces, why couldn't I see them? I saw a flower, a red flower tied against a pale wrist. A corsage, someone from the dance?

The next few minutes, seconds, I had no idea how long this was really lasting and what my body was doing at this time, I was consumed by the vision. Something hit the bonnet, hard, the windshield forked into a million shards that clung to position but threatened to shatter at any moment. The driver hit the brakes, they screeched, the sound piercingly loud, I felt my hands clasp my ears. The car spun round, veering sideways off the tarmac. Then the metal of the car warped and twisted in a terrifying crescendo as the car made contact with a tree at the side of the road. There was smoke coming from the engine, but inside the cab there was only silence. Then it was over.

Same as last time, the first thing I saw was Jake's face.

Horrified he raised a hand to steady me, he hadn't been touching me, so it must have been only a split second. I was grateful he didn't have time to touch me while it was happening, he shouldn't ever be subjected to that.

"Scarlett. Was that what I think it was?" Concern washed all the color from his cheeks; I could feel the vibrations of his trembling hands on my shoulder. I put my hand on his, but I could see it provided little reassurance. He was scared, so was I. I knew I had to find who it was and warn then, how I didn't know; it wouldn't be the easiest thing to explain to someone.

He was about to ask me what I saw, having experienced first-hand the accuracy of my last vision he probably didn't want to be in one of them. The mere thought made my stomach lurch, a sharp contrast to the usual leap I felt there when I was with him.

"Someone here is going to get hurt. A red car, the drive home, there's an accident." I was speaking so quickly I exhausted myself, my breathing erratic. "There isn't much time, it happens after the dance."

"Whoa, slow down. Who was in the car?" He gripped both of my arms in his hands and forced his gaze upon me.

"I don't know, I couldn't see their faces, it was dark, something hit the car and it span off the road, it hit a tree and then it was silent. I couldn't see what happened to them but it didn't feel good." I shook free of him and frantically starting searching the room, pushing people aside trying to spot the red corsage, the one thing I could make out in my mind. There must have been twenty that looked like the one I saw.

I started pulling couples apart in a frenzy. "Did you come here in a red Ford?" Their eyes wide with fear and confusion as I moved on to the next couple. All shaking their heads, answering even though something within them told them to run from the mad girl. Before I knew it the music had dimmed and the room was a sea of eyes fixed on me.

I felt him before I saw him. His hand grabbing my arm, his grip hard and angry. "Miss Roth I think that is quite enough. Have you been drinking?" He glared again. "I suggest you leave before you ruin the evening for anyone else."

"But, they could get really hurt." I lost any concern for the fact what I was saying sounded insane, seemed to me like I should be getting used to it.

His grip tightened, his skin burning mine, but not the way Jake's did. "Son, I think you better drive Scarlett home." He passed me over to Jake forcefully, like he was throwing me in a cell. Jake's touch was soft, calm, he put his jacket over my shoulders and started so steer me towards the door. I writhed free, my arms flailing. "I can't just let it happen Jake." Every pair of eyes fixed on me. He looked down, exhaled and met my gaze. "Scarlett, nobody would believe you anyway, it might be wrong, it's not your responsibility." He pulled the jacket back over my shoulders and led me out the door. As we made the steps I heard the music fade back in and the faint murmur of conversation, no doubt a flurry of theories about what mental disorder the new girl was suffering from.

I kicked the tire of the car, hard, blackening the toe of my satin shoe. "Jesus Jake. They might die. I need to warn them." I stared right at him, expecting him to concede.

"Scarlett, listen to me. Even if we found them." For the first time there was a little disbelief in his voice, like he was thinking the same thing. "Don't you think it's messing with fate, stopping something that is meant to happen?" He was serious, I was stunned.

"I would rather mess with fate than have their blood on my hands." The emotion expanded within me and hot, salty tears started to roll down my cheeks. I suddenly felt so exhausted I could barely stand. I let myself into the car and slumped into the seat. I could feel it was too late, whatever I could have done, and the time had passed.

"Just take me home." I shifted my body, angling it away, facing the window. I didn't look at him once, I couldn't. We pulled up at the house, lights out; Mom was in bed, a small mercy. He flicked the ignition off and turned to face me. He stroked a lock of my hair over my shoulder so he could see my face and ran his finger down my cheek, picking up the track of my tears.

"I didn't mean. I understand what you wanted to do,

but I was protecting you." There was real sincerity in his voice. "Not everyone will understand Scarlett, I don't want them looking at you like some kind of freak." The muscles in my jaw tightened.

"Is that what it is? You're worried to be seen with me now everyone thinks I'm some kind of nut job?" I turned away again, already placing my hand on the door latch. He reached over and pulled it away.

"Is that what you really think? That I am ashamed of you?" He pulled my chin round to face him. I shrugged. He clasped my face in both of his hands, then let go momentarily freeing his right hand to unbuckle his seat belt. Anticipation mixed with my waning anger rose in my chest. He placed his hand back to the spot of my cheek still burning from his last touch, leaning his body toward me he pulled me gently to cover the remaining distance and let his lips find mine. They were slow and careful to start, but gained purpose as he moved against me. Parting my lips with his, he traced the space between my lips with his tongue and my mind erupted with hunger for him.

Though it pained me to pull away and went against every instinct in me, I knew I had to get back to the manuscript, see if it held any more clues. I had to start somewhere. I pushed him gently away with both my hands, even having my hands on his shirt made me feel odd, kind of like I was watching myself, out of my own body.

"Jake I have to go. I'll talk to you tomorrow." I turned

and pushed the door open, I felt him grab my wrist.

"Do you promise?" His voice was pleading, frightened. I smiled. "I am not going anywhere I just need to process this Jake, if this keeps happening like this I need to understand it, focus, you know?" He was looking down, but he nodded. I felt a real vulnerability coming from him; like he was frightened he wouldn't see me again.

It took a while before he spoke. "Ok then. But please, call me tomorrow. I need to know you're ok." He wouldn't let go of my hand until I agreed. With that I let myself out and closed the door quietly behind me, desperate to avoid waking Mom. It wasn't the usual school social story to tell.

My room was dark, colder and more alien than it had been for weeks. I felt the dark, fast moving fear whirling around in the pit of my stomach; I hadn't missed it, not one bit. I tossed my dress, an unwelcome reminder of a disastrous evening, onto the floor and ripped my beads from my neck; tiny pearls cascaded to the floor and rolled in every direction. I slumped into bed and took stock of my nightstand; the once well-thumbed manuscript had been left untouched for weeks. I pulled it onto my bed and propping myself up on one arm I started to flick through, there was little time for romance now, I needed details, what kinds of things did she see? Could she stop them? What happened to her when people found out?

Pages and pages passed; there was little mention of her visions. Had they stopped? Then about forty pages in everything changed, her tone was frantic, fearful and the handwriting was barely legible. I squinted in the dim light trying to make out her words.

The hysteria is spreading, more and more girls are afflicted. No-one is safe. Lilleth Sawyer was the last one to be picked out. They took her from her sick bed, away from her family and stood her up there for all to see. The girls writhed in agony when she stood before them, claiming she was harnessing the powers of evil at that moment to pinch and burn them. Lilleth wept, the questions were leading, the decision already made. Once they named you, time was short. I will stay away from the trials now; being in such proximity will not serve me well. If I were to see something in that room I would be named for sure. I am scared. I mean no harm, in fact I am learning, all the time. I can now to focus on the images, see further and longer. If it were allowed I may even be able to save people. I am no witch.

The entry stopped abruptly at the word witch. The word rattled round in my ears, making the fear squirm and writhe inside me. I scanned a few more pages. It seemed I had, along with a lot of other people completely misunderstood the whole Salem Witch Trial thing. The next few passages made things a bit more clear, I read quickly, hungrily picking out the salient points and watched them jump off the page into my consciousness.

I read on and on. Young girls, whom with hindsight

may have been suffering nothing more than the physiological effects of the times in which they grew up were becoming 'afflicted'. It was these girls who would shape the history of Salem and one of the most famous witch hunts in history. They crawled on all fours, convulsed, screamed. In such a time when the only explanation for these events was the devil's work they were forced to determine the 'witches' who had afflicted them this way. They picked out women whom they claimed had come to them in dreams, whose 'figures' had appeared to them, a sure sign of the devil's involvement. No other evidence was necessary, the visions of these children was enough to damn the women in question. Women were scared, frightened that they would be the next subject of the girls' visions and hauled from their families into the make-shift court.

I read until my eyes were heavy, weighed down by sleep, and intrigue with my 'condition' I pulled the covers over my shoulder and allowed the thought of Jake's lips to wash away the fear and darkness. It was sleep but dominated by lurid, broken dreams. I saw the vision again, I could feel Jake's father's arm on mine, burning, I saw the same, odd anger I had seen in him the first time we met. His touch shocked me and I awoke briefly, the panic raw and hot in my stomach. The similarities were getting harder to ignore.

Another Saturday meant time to read, research. I

pulled on my sweats and packed my bag, I needed to get out of the house, away from Mom and her questions. All I could think as I walked downstairs was about how horrific Monday at school would be. The pointing, the rumours. I had officially ruined my social life here, and probably Jake's too.

"Scarlett, in here, I need to talk to you." Her voice had lost that loving, motherly tone; it was more authoritative, abrasive. I wasn't comfortable with whatever was going to happen, I knew that much.

I trudged, wearily into the dining room to find Mom, glasses perched on the end of her nose, hair twisted into a rough chignon with a pencil in true nutty professor style. Had the atmosphere not been so heavy it may have drawn a smile.

I knew she could sense me in the doorway, her ears had pricked up causing the hair to rise slightly on her head, but she didn't turn.

"Yeah?" I threw back a similar tone, my lack of sleep and the grinding fear and embarrassment did not lend themselves to argument or accusation. Nothing had happened but I could sense the way this was going.

"Mr. Mayer called by this morning." She paused for dramatic effect or to make me feel more dread, if that were possible. Either way it was working.

"Oh. And?" I didn't want to give too much away, though I sensed after last time that the confusingly unpleasant Mr. Mayer being the exact opposite to his son would have relished the opportunity to fill my mom in on my little relapse into lunacy.

"He said there was some kind of problem last night. That you…" Her voice broke off, it wavered and I knew she was fighting the lump in her throat. She composed herself and continued cautiously. If there had been one more person there I would have sworn it was an intervention.

"That you had another..." She chose her word carefully. "Turn?" It was a question, but I had never studied for the 'explain to your mom you can probably see the future' test' I was doomed to fail.

"Mom. I'm fine." I placed my hand on hers where it sat glued to the table, knuckles white, the blue veins highlighting a map across her skin. She was going to butt back in so I made a preemptive strike. "I had one of those weird blood sugar dips, you know I get those. I felt a bit weird and I creeped a few people out, no big deal." I fought so hard to keep an even tone to my voice, the whole time the panic threatened to take me over and turn me into a quivering wreck. I won, for the moment.

She looked back down; she couldn't even bear to meet my gaze. "Either way, he recommended someone." This did not sound good; the darkness growled in satisfaction, it was gaining strength. She pressed her words and her lips. "He thinks it might help you to you know, talk to someone."

My mouth was open; they were staging an intervention of sorts. They wanted to pack me off to a shrink. "I know what you're thinking, it's not a shrink." She always did know how to read my mind, although I was grateful that it was selective.

"He's just a doctor, but he has a great deal of experience in handling the manifestation of stress in teens." She gripped the edge of the table, no doubt bracing herself for my reaction. "I think it sounds like the move could have affected you more than we thought."

"Are you serious?" I was furious and scared. The last thing I needed was any kind of doctor digging round in my head. "Mom. I do not." Emphasis on the not. "Need to see a doctor. The only thing stressing me out right now is the fact you think I do." I was visibly shaking and the fear threatened to knock me down as my legs trembled.

She put her head in her hands and then beckoned me over to her. Putting her hand on mine she finally looked right at me. "I'm sorry baby. I shouldn't even have said anything, I thought it didn't really sound like you." She was stroking my hand now, the way Jake had when he realized what had happened the first time, the comfort was the same, though I would have given anything at that moment to be with him even though I was mad at him.

"Just promise me something." Her eyes pleaded. "That you'll tell me if there is something going on, something bothering you or anything?" I felt guilt knowing I was going to have to look her right in the eye and lie.

"Mom. I swear." Ouch, it hurt. "I am fine, everything is just fine. I am going out now, just going to head down to the library and catch up on some school work." Another lie, I was saddened by how easily it had come to me.

I knew it had worked because she was already back tapping on her laptop. I had gotten past her for now, but if Mr. Mayer insisting on not only being present each time something weird happened to me, but even more annoyingly telling my mom then I was sure to have to face this again soon.

I walked. The car felt too claustrophobic today. It was like there was so much going on in my brain my head could explode at any time. The air I was gasping in through panic stricken breaths was helping a little to ease the pounding. I could feel the corner of the manuscript jabbing my back with each step, I knew there was more in there I needed to see, but I was already creeped out. The same kind of visions as a girl who lived three hundred years before me, a girl who faced persecution for trying to use her 'gift' to help people. The world had changed a lot since then I knew that, but I feared that I may have already stumbled upon those for whom time and history did not equate to tolerance and acceptance.

I hadn't known exactly where the library was when I started out. I wandered a little aimlessly for while hoping the effect of the cold air in my lungs was cumulative and that I would soon feel better.

I found the library pretty easily in the end, turns out I had walked past it before, the time I had crossed paths with Jake, the day I first went mad. It was quiet, as you would expect, but eerily so. There was a female desk attendant who was, also as you would expect, reading. She didn't even look up when I walked in, my sneakers barely making a sound on the parquet floor. The building was another old, impressive one. Its huge ceiling covered in ornate coving and gold leaf. It must have been thirty feet up.

I found a corner between two huge shelves with a small, old desk and I pulled up the chair. I pulled out my manuscript and a little note book. I needed more background. Strangely enough it wasn't too much of a challenge finding books about the witch trials in Salem Library. I piled the books as high as I could manage to carry and see over and put them down on my desk with a reverberating thud, I bet she looked up then, I was grateful I was so tucked away.

I was distracted by two sets of sad, monochrome eyes staring at me from the morning paper which lay discarded on the edge of the desk. CRASH HORROR KILLS TWO. I felt instantly sick; my skin became clammy and crawled. I didn't read on, I didn't have to. I knew the rest. I took a few moments to compose myself; the terrifying accuracy of these visions lay heavy on my mind. My mind was still reeling and my stomach churning as my phone vibrated in my bag. I found it uncharacteristically quickly, Jake. I knew why he was calling. I lay it in my lap until the vibrations stopped, scared to make too much noise. I stared at the screen until the voicemail icon flashed up, one new message. I brought the handset tentatively to my ear and pressed play. A voice normally the source of such calm for me, now frantic and breathless.

"Scarlett. Where are you? Have you seen the news? They're dead, Jesus Christ, you were right, both killed on impact. My dad knows the families. He was asking questions about your behavior last night. I told him you thought the red Ford was being towed and that's why you were asking. Not like he would believe the truth. I'm really sorry for dismissing it like that; I know you wanted to help. Please call me." The message did nothing to allay my feelings of dread. This was real. My visions were real. I had no idea how to process this. I did the only thing that came naturally to me, read. Somewhere in here, this cavernous place walled in books, there must be some answers. Jake would have to wait; I couldn't dissect these events with him now.

I flicked through and through scribbling information down from transcripts, court reports, and eye witness accounts. The whole saga, if that was the right word, was hard to get my head round. The more I took in, the more horrifying it was; how this hysteria marred a generation and how many women were killed. I struggled to comprehend how the words of children had overruled those of previously respected women. The mental images of the accused sobbing, children pointing them out to hoards of terrified people at a time when an idea grew so big, so out of hand, so fast that it destroyed a community and put it in the history books for eternity.

I sat for hours trading each pile of books for new ones. Literally hundreds of people had written historical analysis of the trials, or compiled opinion from learned experts from around the world. I put one of the really heavy going books back; it was huge and just too complex. Its language was full of jargon and its print so small it hurt my head squinting trying to read it.

As I slipped it back on to the shelf I had to maneuver some others out of the way, there really was a ton of information on this stuff. A slim book wedged at the back was stopping me. I reached back, the other books burning the skin on my forearm as I fought to grab it with my fingertips. It had a green cover, but it was blank. It sparked enough intrigue for me to add it to the pile.

By the time I left my notebook was full, I had run my highlighter dry and had to join up to the library so I could take the remaining books home. I hoped if I read some of the historical books alongside the manuscript I could piece together what had really happened all those years ago and what was happening to me. My fixation with the history surrounding my heroine's life was growing rapidly. Everything about the period fascinated me and brought home with each breath the relief that I was not born in that time.

The house was empty when I got home. I took the welcome opportunity to absorb some more witch drama as I shoveled Doritos into my mouth; I had no energy to make real food. As ever I retreated up to my room, it promised me the privacy I needed.

My thoughts were noisy and vivid. I could feel the dread for Monday building inside me. Where the first dark spot had been there was now two, pulsing, threatening to merge and set me mad following last night's drama. I had only hours to come up with a credible cover up, it would be a challenge, even though I had become more of a seasoned deceiver of late. Teenagers were naturally more curious, skeptical and judgmental. However I tried to dress it up I knew I was in for a tough ride.

I took the chance to put my desk to good use. I spread out the books on its glass surface, reminders of my old, simple life smiled back at me. A montage of my pictures and memories immortalizes below the work surface, me and Brooke on our first day as juniors, our first solo trip into Washington and pictures of my holidays with Mom and Dad before the divorce, one at the Grand Canyon on my tenth birthday and another at Disneyland on my eleventh. A smile tried to win over my heavy face but it wasn't strong enough and retreated as I covered the smiling faces with my research.

One thought kept me truly positive, Jake. Though I was still mad at him for his seeming embarrassment I knew if the tables were turned it would have been hard not to feel a little weirded out by that kind of behavior. The reminder of his scent so close to me and the feeling of his lips so forceful against mine by way of reassurance was enough to send shivers down my spine. Goose pimples etched a dot to dot on my skin and I rubbed them rapidly with my hands to warm up.

"Shoot. Jake." I had promised to call. I had wanted to, but I was scared that the embarrassment from last night would swoop in and steal the pleasure from the conversation. I grabbed the phone, my grip tight and punched in his number, memorized already I shook my head at how much of a hook he had in me.

Each ring was a lifetime. I was about to hang up when a familiar but unwelcome voice answered. I should have called his cell, I knew that number too. "Errr....Hi, is Jake home?" My voice was trembling a little, the anxiety was back, and it had brought some friends. My hands shook, I had to steady one with the other to keep from dropping the phone.

The voice replied, measured, monotone. "Can I ask who is calling?" I knew he knew, but I still didn't know why he was so against me. The most he could be worried about was that I was mildly unstable, but he must have been able to see I cared about his son and I didn't think that warranted his consistently cold and bizarre behavior around me.

I took a deep but silent breath before I spoke. It felt cold in my lungs. His breathing was measured and consistent which just highlighted my own erratic pattern. "Mr. Mayer, it's Scarlett, Roth." Just in case his son happened to know another teenage girl with my name who kept seeing the future.

He waited an inhumanly long time before returning the conversation. "Ahh Scarlett." Subtext as I heard it went something like 'ahh unhinged new resident whom I wish had absolutely nothing to do with my son'. "He is... urm just out right now." Then without any further warning or the customary 'Did you want to leave a message' he went. The receiver went dead. The tone taunted me as I sat paralysed with complete shock, what the hell was his problem?

Inexplicably, my eyes were drawn to the huge pile of papers and books on my desk and something I couldn't place burned inside me. I had so much to figure out, the mere thought of what lay ahead exhausted me and I slumped fully clothed onto my bed.

RESPONSE

I hated that for that one moment, for like five joyous seconds I didn't remember what had happened on Friday night, the vision, the staring, the frantic searching thought the sea of scared looking kids, kids who today I would have to see again.

I prayed, which was rare, but I actually prayed that something horrible, major or globally significant would happen so I could avoid my fate. A hurricane, a minor flood, anything but a normal school day tainted with sheer humiliation. The thought of it turned my stomach. The dark patch of fear, which over the last few days had taken up permanent residence inside me flexed its strength and pulled my face into a wince.

I avoided Mom and breakfast; I couldn't take either and decided to walk. The cold air took my breath as I trudged forward, weighed down with fear. I clung to the fact I would see him and he probably, hopefully held enough sway to keep the wolves at bay for the day or possibly even until something else big enough happened and the student population could forget I was a complete mental case.

Her eyes sought me out from across the lot and after a hint of tentativeness Lydia trotted over to me joining me under the shelter of the cafeteria's overhanging roof. The sky had greyed considerably and it threatened rain, maybe the flood thing could happen. Trying to be normal she flashed me a heavy smile as she glanced around to see how many people may have clocked her associating with me.

"Hey. So how was the rest of your weekend?" The sing song tone of her voice was there but today I didn't believe it. She was on edge, completely attuned to the glances of the rest of the kids, shame she couldn't realize they weren't for her.

I put a reassuring hand on her wrist. "Lydia." My voice was direct and it caused her face to drop. "I really appreciate what you are trying to do, and I love you for it. But you don't have to do this. It's not your job to save me." I brought my hand back and shuffled my bag strap back onto my shoulder as I pivoted on my feet to turn away.

I managed to take a step in the silence which I had already taken as relief, she felt free from her obligation, I was surprised not to hear her pumps hitting the tarmac as she ran away in glee like a slave freed.

"Scarlett." Her hand was on my bag; she tugged it lightly and pulled me back to face her. I couldn't look this time, the lump in my throat was throbbing and aching, it promised at some point to overwhelm me, but I was putting up a good fight. She twiddled her bag in her hands as she hung it in front of her and her face was twisted with emotion, though I wasn't able to look long enough to figure out which one.

"Look. I don't know what happened. And I don't know if you wanna talk about it. But whatever happened and whether you do or don't want to tell me, that's cool. I'm your friend." She smiled at me, it was real and I felt overcome again but this time with happiness, she meant it.

She pressed her point and I welcomed the words. "I am on your side. We are on your side me and Taylor." Those few syllables washed over me and I felt empowered, whatever happened they seemed to care enough not to want to ditch me and I was more grateful for their friendship than ever.

I wanted to come back with something a little more profound, it didn't work out, but the sentiment was right where it needed to be. "Thank you. Really." Then like nothing had ever happened, like the Friday, the past few minutes had never happened her face lit up and she grabbed both my hands in hers, eyes wide she grinned a sly grin.

"So... come on. Enough of this diversionary nonsense,

you never really told me much about you and the delectable Jake. I can't take it anymore I need details." The mention of his name had indeed banished my fear and the corners of my mouth turned up into a broad and telling smile.

We talked as we walked and carried on long into Biology. I gave her the edited version, the one without the injured old woman, the weird nonsensically despising father and the twisted old Ford in the dark, that didn't make for a great romantic revelation. I kept in the important parts though; the bits that made me smile like an idiot and shift my eye contact to the grain on the work bench.

"He kissed you, right there in the car?" She was so high pitched I could barely hear her. "Oh my god, his hands on your face? Both hands or one? Did you use tongues?" She was back in machine gun mode and practically salivating with every detail. I tried to reply in a way that would satisfy her near insatiable need for drama and gossip.

"Yes in the car, when he dropped me off after the dance. Yes both hands and yes." We looked at each other and dissolved into hysterics, drawing the attention of more than a couple of our classmates.

Before I knew it the day had passed, and it would have been great, no-one even said anything about the dance, Lydia had shifted her position conspicuously a couple of times when we were talking at lunch, I presume to shield me from some peering eyes, but he wasn't there. I didn't know why, but it became more difficult the more the day went on to hide my concern. My eyes darted around from lunch and I knew Lydia and Taylor knew I was looking for him, there was pity in their eyes, like they thought I might have over imagined the events of Friday, after final period I wasn't sure myself.

The parking lot was different today, less activity. People moved slower, voices were hushed and grief wound through the crowds in whispers and cries. There were flowers and cards littering the grass below the school sign like mournful confetti. Tributes to young lives lost. I felt guilty; the sensation so strong, I should have saved them. I selfishly took some small comfort in the fact people seemed too blinded by their shock and grief that they failed to connect my crazy behavior with the tragic consequences. A girl I recognized from the locker two down from mine was knelt on the damp grass; her arched frame convulsed with silent, pained sobs and I felt my lip tremble with the promise of yet more emotion. Another dark haired girl I didn't recognize helped her to her feet and I stood, paralyzed and watched her walk away leaning as if her legs couldn't take it. She was obviously friends with them, the couple. Another student, a tall guy in a letterman jacket placed a football covered in scrawled condolences at the foot of the posts and placed a hand over his heart as he stood in silence for a moment. I had to get out of here, this was like torture.

Lydia and Taylor's sadness was a little conspicuous by its absence, which made me think either they knew, or just that they felt me too fragile to burden me with any of their upset. It must have been the latter; surely no-one could have figured it out without saying something? Which meant they were just looking out for me; that was so nice it made it almost too hard to bear. I felt like I should scream it at them; my confession, my culpability in this tragedy but I was a coward and knew my weakened mind couldn't handle the outcry. Instead I made my excuses and distanced myself.

I watched them jump into Lydia's mom's Mercedes and waved them off, they had offered me a ride but I wanted to feel the air in my lungs and think, meaning depress myself with theories and hypotheses about Jake's absence. He did bunk from time to time but today was an odd day to choose, just a couple of days after he promised to stick it out with me. I still hadn't spoken to him and any anger I had on Friday had dissipated and was now replaced with concern.

I was becoming a pro at avoiding Mom; she was working so many hours I hadn't had to speak to her much since the time she had tried to send me to a shrink. Though I knew I had the delightful Mr. Mayer to thank for that. I thought about calling Jake again, finding out where the hell he was, but I didn't want to appear desperate, though I knew I was and I would have bet a dollar on the fact he knew I was too.

The phone burned in my hand, the voice in my head taunting me and laughing at me for my weakness, the rings lasted for an eternity, then a familiar voice appeared in my ear.

"Hello?" It sounded so calming and beautiful I couldn't speak right away. I wanted him, needed him, but I was so, so mad and the two conflicting reactions to him battled out in my head for a few seconds before I could speak.

"Hi." I kept my tone reflective of my mood. Then I waited. He said nothing, nothing. There was a hollow and painful silence for a minute.

"Scarlett hi. Urm, is everything ok?" His voice was uneven, possibly a tell that he wasn't as relaxed as normal, but I couldn't make it out, my head too busy to read anymore into his tone. I wanted to hang up, I wanted to so badly, but I knew that I couldn't. My emotions alternated within seconds from completely pissed at him to just being so relieved to hear his voice, like no-one else in the world would have done right then. Soon I was back to pissed just in time to make my move. "Oh, I'm great thanks. After one of the most terrifying and humiliating events in history my boyf..." I paused, crap, what was I about to call him? I suppose that is what he was but we hadn't discussed it and I certainly couldn't assume, today had made that perfectly clear. "Then…" voice quivering, unable to regain the same directness as before I blundered through. "You, after vowing to stick by me and help me make it through the day today, are a complete no show. I tried to call you back after you left that message but your dad said you were out. Where have you been?"

He didn't make a sound, in fact if there hadn't been even a faint background noise at his end you would had thought he had just upped and left the phone dangling there. I was getting edgy, edgier, the silence was crushing me and I was getting uneasy and scared. Mostly scared that I had pushed him away, so far that he might not entertain the idea of coming back to me, the thought of which caused my lungs to seize and sent pains shooting under my ribs.

"I am really, really sorry Scarlett. I was going to call you." He was scared too, why?

"Then why didn't you? I spent all day cowering away from the glares of our entire class. They think I am some complete freak and without you there I started to believe them. I don't know if I can keep going back there, not without you. It was awful, there were all these cards and flowers and all I could think was how it was my fault, how I should have saved them." I twisted my t-shirt material around my finger and watched with baited breath as it turned purple, I was sweating and my heartbeat was so loud I could have sworn he heard it through the receiver.

"I know. And I am so sorry. It was my dad." His

voiced was hushed, almost inaudible, like he was hiding. "He wouldn't let me leave today. He said I had to stay away from the backlash, that I shouldn't be associated with you." My mouth was open, not that I should have been shocked, his father had made no secret at all of how much he disapproved of me, though my behavior in crowded places wasn't helping.

He kept going. "I fought, hard Scarlett, I told him he was ridiculous, but we got in this big fight and he hit me. He has never hit me, ever and he locked me in my room until school was over." Then he waited, eager to know my reaction. This was like a soap opera, people don't say, or do things like that.

"But why? Why does he hate me so much Jake? I need to understand." By this point my lips were trembling and the pains from my chest manifested into a solid lump in my throat.

"He doesn't hate you, he's just hard work. He will come round especially when he realizes..." he paused whether for effect or to get the right words I am not sure, but I was holding my breath again. "When he realizes how I feel about you. Scarlett I would never have left you there today out of choice, you have to believe me. I will be there tomorrow and the next day and all the other days after that, right with you I promise."

I felt awful. The wedge I was driving between them was greater than ever and I knew the right thing to do would probably to release Jake, let him go but I was feeling selfish and greedy for him and I couldn't imagine giving him up. "Thank you. And I am sorry for getting you in so much trouble. I just feel so much safer with you." I heard Mom's key in the door. "I better go. I'll see you tomorrow Jake."

"Night Scarlett." His voice was still hushed; I guessed Mr. Mayer Senior was lurking in the shadows. "See you in the parking lot in the morning."

"Ok, thanks." I was starting to relax, the very thought of seeing him again was delightful, though it was torturous to have to wait till morning.

"And Scarlett..." His voice resumed to normal volume, a gallant move. "Two things. You cannot blame yourself for what happened, it wasn't your fault. I will keep saying that every day until you accept it and second, you better start getting used to calling me your boyfriend." And with that he hung up, quickly, but rather that mourn the end of the call, I was beside myself, grinning like an idiot. Jake Mayer was definitely, officially my boyfriend. Apart from me being completely insane, seeing the future and most of the school avoiding me, I couldn't be happier.

I remained in a state of euphoria for a while, just lying on my bed, staring at the ceiling, I was never going to be able to sleep, not now. I rolled onto my side and picked at threads on my quilt cover, unable to shake the thought of Jake from my mind. I pictured him lying on his bed, sleeping, peacefully and it felt good to be able to think those thoughts, safe in the knowledge I was his girlfriend instead of the dream intruder I had become in recently; hovering over him desperately vying for his attention.

I was about to give in, try sleeping and turn the light off when I spotted some of the unread piles of notes and books I had brought back from the library. They were almost obscured discarded clothes from the weekend, but I felt compelled to dig them out.

The more I read the more I was convinced there would be something in these pages to help me understand who my girl was and what happened to her. When you strip back the candy company façade and plastic black cats, you found a place rich with controversy, passion, secrets, some of them dark and well buried.

I was getting so involved I moved back to the desk, where the original pile of books was still heaped over my scrawled notes. I read pages and pages on the 'believers' those who condemned and named witches, how they acted, what they said and how those with a position of power didn't once stop to consider the consequences of their rash decisions, many of which were just based on fear.

My eyes were starting to betray me, giving way to sleep, but I decided to plough on. I pulled on my slippers and headed downstairs where the glow of Mom working in the dining room filtered into the hallway from under the doors. I crept back moments later clutching a strong coffee, looked like we were both in for a long night. I paused in the leaked light from the room and listened; I could just hear her paperwork and shifting of objects across the table. She let out a sigh and I jumped as if I were an intruder. I was so on edge it was getting ridiculous and I shook my head at myself as I headed back upstairs for peace and some small comfort.

I pawed the pages for what seemed like hours; so much pain and hatred, I couldn't believe what I was reading at times and the reality of what had happened all those years ago came to life in my mind's eye.

I clipped the final page in the pack I was reading against its counterparts and prepared to admit defeat. I picked up the next pack and hesitated; I couldn't give it my full attention now, so I slid the next pile into my book bag and hung it on my door. I couldn't be sure how long it took me to fall asleep, but I know my eyes were closed as I reached for the lamp and dreams of exciting plans with Jake lit my path to a surprisingly deep slumber.

KEY

I had wanted so badly to see Jake before school but my late night research session led to a major oversleep and Mom hauling my quilt from me boot camp style. The half hour that followed was manic to say the least and included one minor coffee burn, a half-eaten bagel and a trip off the front step narrowly avoiding a total face crash. I sent Jake an apologetic text knowing there was no way I could make our parking lot date and went all out with three kisses.

By the time I made it to class I just about had time to visit my locker before a pop quiz on the history of minority groups; irony?

Three long, torturously long, hours passed before I could seek him out. The cafeteria was heaving, throngs of kids fighting for the tots, slurping on soda and making fun of anyone they could to take the attention away from them and their own teenage insecurities.

I felt vulnerable without the girls, while they were trying out to be the next cheerleaders I sat down alone, hoping he would come to me. It was the only way I could be sure it had actually happened. Then he came in. Sauntering across the room his eyes caught mine and he flashed me a secret glimpse of his incredible smile, it was really happening. The real test would come when he reached me, the way he decided to greet me in that moment was going to define our new found relationship entirely. Public displays of affection are not usually a big hit in school, especially in a room with an arsenal of food missiles to hand.

His hand slid across my back and he leaned down, pulling my chin up with a light touch of his finger and kissed me on the lips. Just a subtle kiss, but a full marks kind of kiss and in that second I felt like a celebrity. Everyone was looking, the popular kids, the nerds, in fact I'm pretty sure the lunch lady paused for a second, this was awesome.

The attention was focused on us for the entire time. The other kids were stunned that I had managed to ensnare this fascinatingly gorgeous guy and I fought the urge to stand on my chair and shout how utterly shocked I was too. I could never have predicted this; how happy I would be to have found someone like Jake. But all my good thoughts were always balanced with a helping of fear. I really didn't understand why, just as it seemed life in Salem could be perfect; that all this vision stuff had to happen. I mean, me... why?

I inhaled every moment with him then as I knew it would be tomorrow before I saw him again. I could take the feeling and use it to fuel me through what I expected to be another long session piecing together my mystery.

It occurred to me that I needed to think smarter and cover all the bases, so I pulled the whole 'female problems' with my class teacher in a bid for freedom and he could barely look me in the eye and sent me on my way. It was the last class of the day so it was easy to get a pass. I ducked past the nurse's office and managed to get off the school grounds without being seen.

The library was dead; this was perfect I could do without someone looking over my shoulder while I was working. I picked the computer as far away from sight as possible and took out the notes. I swirled my hair around my pen and used it to pin it up, chignon style so my hands were free to type.

'Real witches in Salem' the keys were light under my fingers and I felt a sense of excitement and anticipation at what I might find out today. The power of the internet plus a table full of testimony would have to lead me somewhere.

Approximately 5,820,000 results. Needle and haystack sprang to mind. Oh I needed to be selective. I skimmed through reams of articles and hear-say, people claiming they were the incarnations of the witches that died in the trials, some living descendants, others saying they commune with their ghosts. There was just so much on the subject, it was blinding. Many seemed to think the start of it all was based on isolation, unrest within the political and religious communities; lack of clear direction and disagreements on what constituted holy, or unholy behavior but at the very heart there were frightened people who just wanted answers.

A significant proportion of the evidence used to sentence the accused was spectral; as in, word taken from those who claimed they saw proof that the Devil was at work in Salem. That itself stirred arguments, with many believing that the Devil could not enter a being without permission, therefore, those pointing the finger, those being afflicted had to have chosen to allow the Devil in. It was mind-boggling. What started with a small group of young girls and accusations of voodoo activities taught by a slave woman became the thing this undisputedly beautiful place was now known for. Salem wasn't even the first place something like this had happened; but the depths of the hysteria and the scale on which the public responded saw this dark period shape the history of investigations into witchcraft everywhere. Just reading it was exhausting and harrowing so imagining those people, how they felt; it was all too much and I felt bad for evening thinking I may be able to relate. They didn't do that to people any more so how bad could it get? Interesting, though none of this was helping me to find out about who wrote the diary.

I lugged my pile of notes onto the desk, her words leapt out from the top of the pile, maybe I needed to know more about her first.

Girls are being taken. I don't know where but they are disappearing. I heard screams from down the lane and there lay two empty chairs in church yesterday. Mother says they are being taken away to be cleansed. I fear they will never return and that I may find myself in their company if my secret were to be discovered. I'm scared; I feel the darkness all around the town, the weight of forces bearing over all we do. Even my words here on these pages pose a threat to my safety.

Taken where? Who by? I typed a combination of search terms trying to find one that would shed even the tiniest bit of light on this information. I tried so many I could barely remember what I had been looking under when something caught my eye. Danvers Psychiatric Unit, Danvers MA. It made sense I suppose to brand people as insane, it gives people in power a label to control people with. Clicking into the link it was a newspaper article from the Massachusetts Guardian, written in 1975.

CLOSURE CONFIRMED FOR INFAMOUS FACILITY

The state office has confirmed that the much maligned Danvers Psychiatric Unit is set to close after more than

120 years. Plagued by reports of poor care and misdiagnosis the 350 bed hospital, which has operated at less than half capacity for more than a decade is being closed down; all remaining residents are being re-homed into other facilities within the month.

Since 1800's DPU has been associated with the treatment of a host of psychiatric disorders and received referrals from all across the state. In 1959 its reputation as a care facility came under fire following at least three complaints that patients had been experimented on and were receiving unorthodox and inhumane treatment at the hands of Chief of Staff Dr Edward Sutcliffe.

Sutcliffe denied the claims and following a brief suspension returned to his post without charge.

The building is set to be demolished within the year unless a suitable buyer can be found. No one was available for comment.

I am not sure what this related to but it showed up for a reason. I clicked print and stashed the pages into my bag.

Turns out the internet is pretty full of information about witches and their ill treatment over the years. I must have gathered another sixty pages before calling it a night.

The light was dimming by the time I set off home and my phone was vibrating furiously in my hand; it was Mom I knew she was worried but I just didn't feel like speaking to her, she would want to ask about Jake and he was my secret, I was scared if I talked too much about it that it would all come undone.

On way home, see you soon. S. x. I know people complain about the use of texting in place of conversation, but I for one welcomed it.

It seemed to take me hours to walk home; my legs were heavy and my eyes tired. I was stirred from my zombie daze as I noticed a car in the driveway; I didn't recognize it and my mom never did anything but work so I couldn't imagine it being a new BFF.

I tentatively let myself in to the sounds of muffled voices in the kitchen. I could hear the chink of a spoon in a mug and the scent of freshly brewed coffee wafted temptingly through. It was a man. Who the hell would my mom have in our house?

I pushed the door slowly open and peered through like a naughty kid, two sets of eyes looked up at me. I froze and the feeling I had almost dared to forget about spread through my chest and hit my stomach like a lead weight.

"Oh hey sweetie. Mr. Mayer just dropped by to check on you after the, err incident the other day. Isn't that nice?" Even my mom gave the impression she thought it was weird to have him sat in our kitchen. She didn't know the guy and he and I shared a mutual dislike of each other.

He sat there, a casual hand holding a mug and just flashed me a short, forced smile. He looked like someone from the past, still wearing his long dark mac unbuttoned over a three piece suit. How dare he come to my house after the way he looked at me, treated me and Jake for that matter? The sadness in Jake's voice when he had told me about his dad hitting him flooded back into my mind and I was furious. My blood boiled with rage and I tried to imply it with a firm stare.

"Hi Scarlett. How've you been doing? Anymore episodes?" He over pronunciated the words emphasizing 'episodes' like he was trying to brainwash my mom into calling it that. He was a nasty piece of work and it was all the more confusing that I had no idea what on earth the motivation was for his odd behavior. He crossed his legs nonchalantly while he spoke and his gaze switched between me and my mom. I could have sworn he was sneering at me. His eyes spoke a thousand words and while I couldn't decipher his intentions entirely, it was clear he was enjoying the tension his presence was stirring in me. I could literally feel my muscles contracting and tightening.

I fixed myself a drink while I answered, I thought it best not to make any more eye contact now than necessary, it could take hours to warm my soul after a few minutes in his company.

"No." I was perhaps a little defensive and short. "I hardly think it really counts as an episode. I'm just exhausted since the move. You know, finding it harder to get a good night's sleep in new surroundings."

My mom was uncomfortable with my tone; her eyes were boring holes in the back of my head. I was never rude, not normally, but this man had behaved horribly towards me for no reason since the first time he met me and I didn't like him, not one bit. I tossed the spoon from my coffee into the sink resulting in a clattering sound; my mom couldn't take much more of the escalating atmosphere, which probably seemed a little unnecessary to her, with her not knowing what a horrible human he was.

"Scarlett. Please don't be so defensive. Mr. Mayer is a Doctor, he is just making sure you are not feeling too stressed. The move has been a big deal. No one would blame you for feeling a little, well, overwhelmed." She focused on my eyes hard, urging me silently to be the polite, well-mannered daughter she was used to. I couldn't do it. Not even for her. This man dared to come into my house and infiltrate my own mom's thoughts and feelings. I could tell he had gotten to her, she was worried about me. No doubt he had fabricated some additional twists to make recent events sound even worse. How on earth someone so disagreeable cold have fathered someone as perfect and caring as Jake was beyond me. The mild similarities in their faces were where it stopped; other than that it was barely conceivable that they shared DNA.

I was torn between rage and a bizarre, lingering fear. The emotions were so fierce they seemed to be almost visible; my vision shrouded in a dark swirling fog of complex reactions to his proximity. It felt like something in my very soul was urging me, willing me to leave. I needed to leave.

The dark frightened space in me whirled with vigor and my stomach lurched. In that moment I did the only thing I thought was safe; I calmly put my coffee down and walked out the room at speed, slamming the door and taking the stairs two at a time to make it into the sanctuary of my bedroom. I locked the door, something I had never even considered before but as long as he was here I wasn't letting my guard down, it wasn't safe.

Their voices could still be heard, but only as low, suspicious, conspiring murmurs. He must have stayed for another half hour before I heard the front door latch the car in the driveway start with a ferocious roar. Its lights fanned across my ceiling through my open curtains before disappearing, taking the sound of the engine with them. He was gone. Though this lightened the feeling I was carrying it didn't remove it. He had taken away my sense of security in my own home. How my wonderful kind, supportive Jake could have been spawned from that man I had no idea. Guess sometimes the apple not only falls from the tree, it rolls away from it entirely, and thankfully that seemed to be the case with the Mayers.

My bag vibrated, I fumbled through the abyss for my phone and exhaled when I saw his name on the screen. It seemed like days since I had seen him, though in reality it was a matter of hours, eventful though they were.

Missed you this afternoon. What did you get up to?

Rumor has it you skipped last period? Tut, tut new girl, already slacking! J xxx

I text back which started a flurry of conversation, he made me laugh, several times and I was happy while it lasted. He signed off saying his dad was back and he had to go and I was willing to bet he had no idea that his dad was returning from terrorizing me and turning my own mom against me. I realized I was being a tad dramatic even in my own head, but that was the way I felt. There was something so off about him.

The sadness I experienced at our communication ending was coupled with dread, my seemingly ever present companion, as I heard my mom heading upstairs. The floorboards in this house were temperamental to say the least; they certainly weren't suitable for sneaking about; if you were lucky and really thought about it maybe. That was the teen in me, making sure I always had an escape route, Mom had clearly never given it so much thought. My ears traced her from the top of the stairs to my door; she didn't knock, or even call out. She waited for maybe a whole minute before moving down the hall towards her own room and quietly latched the door closed.

I was not at all likely to sleep so I heaved my now bulging and impossibly heavy book bag onto my unmade bed. I tipped it out rather haphazardly and suddenly my quilt was awash with history, supernatural and otherwise.

The copies of the diary were now beyond well manhandled, like a favorite story, only I suppose with a less than happy theme. A series of annotations followed the last entry, presumably by the first person to study them.

It appears there have been several pages removed from the original document. Initial examinations lead us to believe there is a gap of at least two months at this point. Whereabouts of these pages are unknown.

Interesting, how irritating to find out I was missing information, what if those pages held the key to what happened to her or what was likely to happen to me? Well there was only one way to find out, pick up from the next available entry and hope.

I haven't seen him since they accused the daughter of the family living nearest us. I can't be sure if this is his choice or not, maybe I am suspected that they think it's contagious and I pose a risk having lived in such proximity. He could have been warned away. Whatever the reason it would give me little comfort; I long for him, my heart aches and I fear I may never see him or hold him again, especially if they find out. What will become of me if they do is starting to become frightfully clear. Though I cannot be sure, and mother and father will protect me as much as they can, I have heard people whisper, talk of hangings, the afflicted being put upon by giant stones and crushed to death. I will take my own life before I allow them to take it from me. Though for now at least I have to hope and pray I am safe. I have had no significant visions in some time, a small mercy.

I felt like I knew what was coming, but reined in my thoughts, I could be wrong after all, I so badly wanted a happily ever after for her. I felt like I wasn't learning as much as I had hoped, she wasn't leading me to any answers about my visions, how I could stop or control them. In my frustration I began skimming, searching for that one thing that could help me. I pulled out a highlighter and scribbled over the odd word, a place name or a family name to Google later. After another half an hour I was losing my reserve of patience and decided to throw it in for the night. I did some frantic highlighting before transferring my papers onto the desk. I knew this was getting interesting but I had no idea where it was going and I had neither the energy nor the will power to fight sleep anymore. It had been a weird day and I was already prepared to trade it for a new, hopefully more pleasant one.

CONNECTIONS

I was finding it increasingly difficult to combine normal teen life with my newly assumed role as psychic/private investigator. Weird how one small (future vision related) thing can happen and all of a sudden nail varnish, hot fashion tips and school drama become less and less engaging. Though one thing seemed to transcend all of that; throw a little Jake Mayer into the mix and everyone was interested, especially me.

I had no option but to face Mom in the morning I sauntered into the kitchen like all was perfectly normal and the air of tension seemed to have dissipated; grabbing the orange juice I pulled out a chair and slumped into it without attempting eye contact.

Mom still hadn't spoken. An unwelcome guest, the tension crept back in like a runaway vine, entangling itself around my nervously tapping feet threatening to trip me up if I made a move. I looked up and she was leaning against the counter, arms folded staring straight at me.

"Can you please explain to me why the HELL you thought it was acceptable to treat Mr. Mayer the way you did yesterday?" She wasn't kidding. Mom rarely shouted, so when she did you knew it was serious. She was buttering her toast but it was like some kind of massacre; she was hacking at the bread, forcing out her frustration through gritted teeth.

"Mom, I know you think you have him all worked out and that because he's a doctor he's all about doing good, but you're wrong about him." As soon as I had closed my mouth I realized that needed qualifying, it didn't make sense without putting into the wider context with all its complex details.

"Scarlett, the man came all the way over here just to check you were ok. It seems he has been there for you a couple of times since we moved and you have to concede your behavior on those occasions was enough to give anyone cause for concern." She looked away, facing out the window onto the river and beyond. If we hadn't been arguing we would probably have been in the process of agreeing how beautiful it looked in the morning sun's glow.

"I wondered how long it would take to come back to that, you secretly thinking I'm nuts." She spun round; I held her gaze in an act of defiance that I knew would shock her.

"I don't…" She shook her head without finishing what she was going to say turned to face away again.

"You know what Mom; I don't have time for this and I don't want to fight with you. Let's just agree to disagree where Mr. Mayer is concerned. I have my own experiences of him and I don't like him, not at all." With that I scooped up my bag and walked out the room. "And you know what?" My voice carried, angrily from the hall, "It would be really cool if just once you trusted me, and listened to me over him." She didn't try to respond or follow me; she just stood still, silent. I knew she would be hurting, I could count on one hand the amount of times we had so much as raised our voices, it didn't happen. I also knew she would be blaming herself for bringing me here, convincing herself I was having some kind of breakdown. God knows what he had told her, the facts would sound damning on their own but I was willing to bet he had embellished the tale and blinded her with some medical theory.

It happened when I was just about to step off the drive onto the sidewalk; everything went wobbly, as if I was watching the world through a veil of water, from the bottom of a deep pool. My stomach lurched like it had both times before, and the light drained from my vision and I could see a room. It was dimly lit and there were low, muffled voices. I could make out at least five people sat round a table but their words were obscured, their hunched body language suggesting it was intentional. They passed something around between them, notebooks? Then it was over.

This one made no sense, it was so brief and nothing happened, all the others seemed more significant, like a warning. I made out no faces, couldn't see what they were looking at or where they were.

I had been rooted to the spot. I spun round to check no-one was around, mostly that Mom hadn't been watching from the house, no sign of her. I set off as if nothing had happened; amazing how quickly you can accommodate change, I hardly even acknowledged a minor premonition these days. Yeah, totally normal school day stuff.

What was meant to be a study hall session turned into a catch up on emails session instead. I regaled Dad, who no doubt was now in cahoots with Mom on the whole thinking I am going mad thing. I was careful to share as much mundane information as possible. I knew he would be looking for chinks in my armor so I poured out every nuance of my life in stereotypical teen style hoping his head would be filled with images of the old me, the one before all this. I followed one email with another, this time to Brooke. I watched as all the most intimate details of my encounters with Jake filled my screen, just reading those facts was enough to make a warm flush spread from my neck up to my face. I had definitely neglected her since I moved and I felt bad for it, but so much seemed to have happened for me, I was starting to find it hard to relate to my old life at all. Plus, if I had tried to tell her it would have only added another ally to Mom and Dad's team for sure. I knew how it looked and sounded, even I was tempted to think I may just be a lunatic. She was probably round at my dad's now, planning the intervention.

The clock moved impossibly slowly, two hours before lunch and Jake and the girls, mostly Jake. I managed to print off a little more research before it was time for my next class.

Dutiful friend and daughter roles complete, history blitzed and now only a two minute walk stood between me and a guaranteed high from Jake's intoxicating smell.

He was already in the lunch room when I arrived. I was sure I could smell his scent lingering in the busy air. His back was arched over the table; he was scribbling something in a pad with his textbooks laid out in front of him, not a lunch tray in sight.

I crept up and traced the line of his spine through his t-shirt with my index finger, something which felt uncharacteristically hands-on for me in a public setting, but I couldn't help it. Touching him brought a whole new world of sensations to me and there was the added benefit of the distraction factor.

He hunched his back up to his neck as I reached his hairline, and without looking back reached up for my hand and pulled it round his neck. Neither of us even concerned for the growing interest in our lunch room liaison.

I slid into the seat next to him and inhaled his being. He stared back at me and closed a couple of his books as he grabbed my hands with one of his.

"So Miss Roth…have you missed me?" Before letting me answer he followed with "Because I've missed you. Pretty worrying really, I was only studying to stop me pining." With that a wry smile lifted the corners of his mouth; that smile, and like a magnet I was drawn to him. I offered only a soft, swift kiss as I was learning to enjoy the desire for more.

"I think you can take that as a firm yes." I could do nothing but smile back, as following my other impulses would have been extraordinarily unlike me and would probably have gotten us both expelled.

"So what did you and your mom do last night, was she working again?"

I pulled a soda from my bag and plucked the ring pull musically while I thought about whether or not to tell him.

"Actually. When I got home last night after being at the library your dad was there." I paused and met his gaze. He closed the one remaining open book with a loud thud and shifted the whole pile to one side as he processed what I had said.

"At your house?" The warmth in his eyes now just a void. I couldn't tell what it meant but I didn't like it, that one glance had stripped me of all my teenage impulses. I didn't even get chance to respond, though the answer was probably too obvious to warrant a reply.

"Jesus. Scarlett I am so sorry. What did he say? Is your mom pissed?" He fired a series of frantic questions at me and pulled my hands back across the table, entwining the fingers from his right hand in mine.

"I'm not really sure what he wanted. I might have been a little defensive." I lied; I was more than a little defensive. "I think he was just checking to see if I was ok." I ended my testimony there, I didn't want to go into how he had stared me down, the creepy way I felt he was trying to influence my mom's thoughts about me; it couldn't lead to anything good.

Then something I didn't expect; "He needs to stop this." And with that, his face all weighted with tension he stood bolt upright, towering over my seated frame and without so much as a kiss stormed through the masses and out the same door in which I had first seen him walk through. The walk had more purpose, but it didn't have the same allure. This time it was all anger.

My mind screamed at me to run after him but even my feelings about his father rooted me to my chair; under no circumstance was I going to initiate contact with him. So I sat, anchored to my seat with thoughts of what would follow and felt a familiar shift; the butterflies that loved Jake so were replaced with a grey longing and anxiety.

Taylor and Lydia saved me not long after; bombarding

me with mindless gossip and tales of the teenage drama kind from cheerleading tryouts; which incidentally sounded more of a brutal bitchfest than even my imagination could conjure and that was saying something because city girls really knew how to dish it out.

When the sands of time finally conceded that the school day must end I was a wreck. I had spent the previous two hours secretly checking my phone under the desk, nothing from Jake. I didn't like this at all. Surely his dad wouldn't hurt him? I didn't know; I found it hard to contemplate, but it was possible.

I left the parking lot on foot, and pulled my coat collar up to shield my ears from what had becoming a blistering cold. As the crowds dispersed onto buses, cars or as swarming throngs onto the streets beyond the school perimeter I knew I couldn't go home. The thought of going there, to Jake's house and seeing him would normally have sent my heart into overdrive, a tantalizing combination of lust and longing but under these circumstances dread took their place.

I hadn't been to Jake's house but I knew where it was, we drove past it the night of the dance and I was grateful for that memory even if the rest was a catastrophe. It wasn't far but I seemed to have out walked the rest of the school kids and found myself heading down his road alone; eerie to go from such chaos to dead calm within a second.

The street was idyllic suburbia, the house was larger

than the ones that neighbored mine, you could see these were the great and the good of the community, the lawyers, doctors and so on. Well-kept lawns were fenced in and bordered by tidy shrubberies and well-to-do cars like Jake's were parked in twos on most of the driveways.

1388. That was it. The car I had seen in my own driveway was parked here, so I was sure about two things; I had the right house and Mr. Mayer was home. There was a screen door separating me from the main house entrance, I tentatively let myself through the first defense and knocked on the door. I waited for what seemed like an eternity but no-one came.

My heart raced and my mind ran away with me, ridiculous and unlikely scenarios pushed me to the brink of hysteria. I pushed back through the screen and took a step onto the drive. Looking up at the house with its white boarded frontage and well-dressed windows it may have looked to an outsider that I was casing the joint, loitering with intent. There was no sign of life. I moved timidly down the side of the house just to check there were no other clues to Jake's whereabouts. There was a double garage at the end of the drive and for a moment I envisaged a young Jake excitedly rooting around for his bike on a summer's day. My daydreams were shattered by a sound. Voices. They were low and largely undistinguishable but they were coming from the garage.

I backed up to the wall and edged my way round the

side. There was a side door neighbored by a small window. I felt sick and I could hear my own heartbeat louder than anything else; the sheer force of my fear pushed it to rattle my chest and I scrambled for my breath, I shouldn't even be here. I cupped my hand over my mouth to conceal the sound of my breathing. I was sure one of the voices was him, Mr. Mayer; it sounded the same as I had heard coming from my own kitchen, my sense of violation from that day rose to the surface and momentarily boosted my confidence as the anger in me was awoken. I situated myself below the level of the window and pushed myself up as slowly as possible to ensure I remained unseen.

I held my breath entirely, still not knowing why I was so scared. As the room passed into view I stared in from my hiding spot, fighting nausea and flashes of white hot panic that spread from the base of my neck right down to my feet. By that point I knew it was him I heard. He was sat at a table, flanked either side by a handful of others. Five of them in total. The room was bare, just the table and two old filing cabinets; a makeshift meeting room.

This was it. My vision. It was this room, these people and it wasn't notebooks it was files. I kept myself out of view, the voices were still too quiet, I couldn't make out what they were saying though it all seemed much less sinister than I was anticipating.

I was about to move away and get back to my search for Jake when I felt a jolt, something touching my skin. I span round with an audible gasp.

"What are you doing here?" He stared straight at me, his voice hushed and hand still firmly on my shoulder.

"Oh my god... you scared the life out of me. I was looking for you. I was so worried when you stormed off I didn't want you in some kind of trouble at home. And as I haven't heard from you all day... I..." he interrupted, grabbed my hand and led me away from my secret spying spot and we went through the back door into the kitchen. He guided me onto a stool at the breakfast bar and before he continued placed a gentle, warm kiss on my cheek. I was exceedingly glad it was him the found me rather than one of Senior Mayer's meeting buddies. That would have been awkward.

"I'm sorry I didn't call. It's been a weird day. I laid into my dad about him visiting you. He just gave me all the usual it's my responsibility as a doctor crap. Needless to say I didn't get very far but I won't let him make you feel like that, especially in your own home." He was stroking my hand while he spoke and I had been trying to focus on his words rather than the feeling of his skin on mine, it was as challenging as ever.

"But anyway...tell me why I find you spying on my dad in my back yard?" He smiled, he was joking and it seemed like it might over complicate things to explain his dad's meeting was the latest in my usually disturbing series of visions.

"I was looking for you. And I heard voices. I didn't want to just barge in so I thought I would just take a peek, in case you were in there…" It didn't sound normal even with my own edits. My curiosity was still burning, I wanted to know what the bizarre Mr. Mayer was doing hiding away with his no doubt weirdo friends in garage. He was still smiling, obviously getting used to me and my weird ways.

"So… what is going on in there?" I realized as soon as I closed my mouth that I really had no right to ask that. He was stood up now, pouring juice. I was fixating on the line of his arm, tracing it with my eyes up to his shoulders. I found myself suddenly behind him, my arms wrapped themselves round his waist and I inhaled him.

His body tensed beneath me and if I didn't know better I would have said I was making him nervous. His hands wound between my fingers and as he started to speak his voice reverberated through his back and sang into my ears.

"Oh. It's as dull as it gets. Every week my dad holds a committee meeting here so all the great and good can come and make decisions on all the things that matter in this town, according to them. I avoid it at all costs, not that I'm allowed anywhere near, it's strictly business. Been going on as long as I can remember."

That seemed reasonable enough. I felt stupid for being so uptight in the first place and being caught hunched below a window spying on my boyfriend's dad; well that was a new low.

He span round and pulled me into him, we lost the next few minutes before we moved into the sitting room and folded into the worn but squishy leather couch. There were two, one against the wall to the kitchen and another against the long back wall which led to the hallway door. The room was warm and lived in but felt distinctly masculine, no photos, no magazines, just books and largely vast spaces on beige walls.

A burst of curiosity took me over and I spoke, quite possibly out of turn without a thought. "Where's your mom Jake?" It had come out sounding like I was a cop, interrogating him, blaming him for her absence. I noticed a slight tension move through his cheekbones and he exhaled audibly, preparing himself to answer. I knew I had made a mistake.

"She... er. She died, when I was three." His eyes, heavy, looked down. I felt guilty for prying and worse for making him talk about it. The sight of him in pain was almost unbearable.

"Jake, I am so sorry. I didn't know...I mean I shouldn't have asked." I placed my hand on his and he smiled.

"No, it's totally fine. I just realized I haven't thought about her in a really long time and that just makes me sad you know? I don't even remember her properly. Sometimes I can catch the scent of a perfume which I am sure is hers and sometimes if I try really hard I can see her face."

"But you must have pictures right?" My disbelief that anyone could be robbed of their memories was obvious. I had it so lucky and half the time I was too busy bitching and moaning to realize it. I made a mental note to give Mom a hug when I got home.

"Nuh uh. Dad flipped out when she died and destroyed them all. He says he couldn't take it, seeing her face. So he burnt them. I do have one, my gramps gave it to me before he died and I keep that one hidden so he isn't tempted to take that one too."

If my feelings about Mr.. Mayer weren't already fully established, then they were now. I know I didn't know what it was like to lose a wife, but to deny a child the memories of his mother knowingly, that was cold. I felt like I could have guessed what she would look like and how much her feminine touch would have made their home completely different. I liked to think she wouldn't hate me the way he did. That maybe we would have gone shopping together and she would have trawled through all Jake's baby pictures to show me while he looked on, embarrassed.

Sensing the time for this talk was over and too much of a wrench for him I leaned over and kissed his forehead. His hands wound into mine and he squeezed them so hard. He was thanking me, with a silent, wonderful thank you for knowing him and knowing when enough was enough.

The sound of a door latching made us both jump and

pull away from each other. "You need to leave, now. It's my dad, they're done. Go out the front now, go. I'll call you later." He shunted me from the couch. I nodded. I had had my fill of time in the company of Mr. Mayer lately, I wasn't about to put myself through anymore. I moved quickly, glancing at my surroundings as I went, Jake had a nice home.

Despite yet more weirdness and paranoia, I was clinging onto the feeling of my time with Jake, it stood out as far more significant than anything else from the day. I was in love with him; there was no room for any other explanation and no point trying to dress it up in any other way. I had fallen as far as it was possible.

A TRUTH

On finding the house empty as usual I took it as my signal to get stuck into my research again. I still had all the hospital stuff, the weird word that I had found and the journal to piece together.

My room was cold, even with the heating on. If you focused hard you could just trace the path of your breath across the space in front of you. I pulled the curtains closed and pulled a sweater over my t-shirt as I made my self comfortable at my desk for the evening. I couldn't help but stare at my photos; my life with Brooke, and of course my dad. Maybe it would be simpler if I had stayed there; I didn't have visions there, I had loads of friends, I could dress how I really wanted. Then a thought seared my mind like a hot poker, the trade off to having all that back would be living without Jake. But he trumped all of that, which made me feel guilty, a pain pushed into my core, but it was true. I would rather be here than anywhere else if he was with me. I wasn't sure how I got this far into it in a matter of weeks, but it was very real. He made me feel alive, safe and at home.

My bag was starting to look like it could rupture at any time; lifting it was starting to get hard too. I made a vow with myself not to collect anymore literature before I had thoroughly gone through what I already had.

I tapped my pencil rhythmically between my fingers daunted by the task ahead; I flicked the stereo on in a bid to get myself more fired up. My phone beeped. It was Jake.

You looked amazing today by the way. Can't wait to see you at school tomorrow. English has become my favourite subject since you showed up. J x x x

I couldn't help but smile and I must have stared at his words on the screen for a good minute. I needed to rein it in a little, I think if he could see into my head and see how crazily I was running away with this thing between us he would run for the hills.

I reached into my bag with a view to picking up where I left off in the library, which seemed as good a place as any. With my bag on my knee I rifled through for the notes in question. They were wedged at the bottom of my bag, blocked by a small thin book, the same one that had gotten in my way the other day. I had totally forgotten about it. There were no markings on its green outer cover at all and a glance inside revealed it had no library markings or stamps at all.

I gently folded back the cover, which was followed at first by a series of blank pages. As I moved through the sheets of warn, weathered paper my eyes caught a glimpse of where the text began. I parted the book there ready to see what this next part of the adventure held for me. Handwriting, in ink, but it was faded in parts. I braced myself; it seemed there was never any telling what would happen next in this town or what nightmares or mystery could lay within the pages of a book.

There was a date etched inside the front cover. This was more modern history than the rest of my recent reading material. I felt a flutter of excitement mixed with trepidation, this could be the one that helped me, gave me answers. What I knew I was looking for was a way to make them stop, but I daren't even admit that to myself, I was worried even allowing the thought to enter my head would make it impossible for it to ever happen. I pushed the thought away, buried it deep along with all my anxiety, fear and the lingering darkness that moved within me when I thought about how my life had been turned upside down by my visions.

December 1991

I can only assume the fact you are reading this means they managed to find me.

The writing was hurried, as if whoever wrote it knew they didn't have much time. I was ready to find out, I had to be.

My name is Alice Markham. I live in Salem MA. When I was four years old I started having premonitions. Sometimes they meant nothing, but they changed and soon I was seeing dark, terrifying visions that I couldn't control.

I put my hand to my mouth, she was describing my life, it was the same as my mystery lady in the journal I had been reading. Seems like whatever was happening to me I certainly wasn't alone.

The older I got the more frequent my visions became and I could no longer keep them a secret. My parents tried everything they could to rid our family of the 'curse' they saw blighting it. Nothing worked. We met a Doctor who said he specialized in this kind of delusion, that's what he called it. He befriended my parents, they trusted him. Blinded by ignorance and a desperate need to be rid of my problem they entrusted me to his care. In 1955, when I was 14 my visions had become so frequent and traumatic that I was unable to hide them, always showing me terrible accidents, deaths and misfortune. He used his influence over my parents to manipulate them into accepting his version of the truth, that I was not of sound mind and I must be committed for my own safety. They agreed and signed the papers the day before I turned 15.

I grabbed a pad of post-its and scribbled as much of the salient detail as I could onto the neon sheets, littering them over my desk like literary confetti. Captivated by this quite frankly terrifying account I was unable to break away, I flicked the stereo off, this needed my full attention.

The hospital was famous, or infamous for its treatment of the insane, so I was terrified to be thrown into this mad house at 15 years old. No visitation for three months minimum, again, all for the greater good. My parents, to my horror, agreed to that too. I screamed, begged, pleaded and splintered my fingernails grasping at the floorboards when they came for me. Naturally, and I realize now, I did him a favor, made it look like I really was mad. I knew I wasn't insane, not that I thought seeing the future was normal, but I had at least heard of others who had the same, shall we say issues.

Danvers was full to capacity. Its patients ranged from the depressed to the unquestionably deranged, I did not fit the line up at all, but I met two who were in the same boat, this is my truth dear reader. You may find this a gift or a curse and if it's the latter I can only apologize, but it must be known and I pray you can deliver it to a more accepting world in my absence.

My throat lurched. I half toyed with putting it down, I had a curse of my own and someone else's was not a burden to carry lightly at this point. I drew in a deep and pensive breath, letting it out slowly through my mouth as I forced my gaze back to the page. If it was fate that brought me here, to Salem, to Jake, to this book then I had no choice but to continue down this path.

Aida and Betty. They sought me out, they could spot it a mile away. Aida was like me in almost every way, most importantly she had the same abilities shall we say. Her story mirrored my own with frightening accuracy, the start of the visions, the family concern the concerned doctor turned petty abductor. Betty was different, she didn't see the future, she was a 'listener' she could hear thoughts, single people out in a crowded room, choose a conversation and focus on its every detail. Once it came out what she could do her father forced her to see him, she tried to tell her family about him, what he was thinking but like my own protests, they only served to incriminate her mind, rendering her a prisoner in Danvers from the age of 16. Now 20 she had heard Aida's thoughts across a communal room and they had been inseparable ever since. The three of us were an interesting team and it wasn't long before our attachment to each other was noted and he separated us on a permanent basis; we were too powerful together. Driven by fear of something he did not understand he abused his power in the blackest way possible. Danvers became a grave for Aida, his tools and machines could not unlock the secrets of her power but they did break her body and her spirit. I watched her deteriorate into one of them, the blank, lifeless faces that place was known for. The colors in her skin faded to grey, the lights in her eyes dimmed and she vegetated until Betty could no longer hear anything, she had gone.

The writing smudged, I lost a few words in an inky whirlpool as my tears landed on the page. This hospital, if you could call it that, had been experimenting on people with gifts like mine. Ordinary people were being tortured and maimed so some doctor could learn more about the human mind. I felt sick and terrified; the only small comfort I found was knowing that nowadays I would be more likely to bank a million making predictions on YouTube than be institutionalized.

This had been going on for decades, people coming in under false pretenses, their fall into lunacy or a sad death masked with medical jargon and families consoled with the knowledge they had been in the best possible place, so they had been led to believe.

I am one of the lucky ones; I escaped with my life, what was left of it. Almost three years to the day a chance arose and we took it... a small human error gave us a chance at freedom and we ran, like we had the strength of a race horse within us, our hands intertwined and we didn't stop. Security had been lax as all wardens were restraining a particularly violent resident having an episode and we didn't even speak; we instinctively took that chance together. Beyond the perimeter we couldn't stop running, terrified we would be caught we ran until our bare feet bled and over exertion made us nauseous. Clinging to each other we wept for hours, tears of joy, relief, fear and loss for our friend. The next hours, days and weeks we lived tormented, terrified. We knew we couldn't go home, ever, we must begin again. We called each other different names; I became Maggie Eagling, a character from one of my favorite childhood books and she became Annie Stowell.

We built a life working in hotels and lodges; we got food and board and cut our hair short so we would not be recognized. Despite our unity in those moments it was not long before the strain of our circumstance forced us apart, we parted company. We were each too much of a reminder for the other to take and only three short months later, Betty headed off in a ride she hitched, headed to Boston, and I tried my best to build some semblance of a life. I spent years living just 10 miles from where my family had lived. I took the risk on more than one occasion of being caught by creeping to the house in the pitch black night to see my father read before bed or glance at my mother looking at my photo longingly. I don't know what he had told them about me, they may think I was dead, missing, still locked up in there for all I know but it wasn't safe for them to know about me I knew that much. As I write this I am 50 years old.

They have been tracing me, I have seen them coming. Please, find someone you trust and lead them to the truth, people need to know what happened there, or people like us will never be free.

A. Markham x

Weighed down by confusion I brought the book to my chest and held it tight as I fell into the quilt on my bed. I wracked my brains; the responsibility of perhaps being 'the one' she spoke of the one who knew the truth and could share it was huge. I didn't know what to tell anyone, or who to tell even if I did. There must be something I was missing here. 'People like us will never be free'. How did she know the person reading it would have the same powers? My mind whirled like oil across water; shifting and changing direction with every second.

A cursory flick through the remaining pages offered something by way of the answers I had been so desperately seeking. Alice's handwriting curled from a noticeably more relaxed hand than the text I had just read. Why me? The question I had pushed to the back of my mind was addressed in the page of a notebook from a total stranger. Though the more of her words I read, the more I felt an affinity with her. By her reckoning the gift always arrived to its victim? Recipient? Whatever we were, as teenagers. The surges of hormones combined with a trigger; stress, anxiety, even significant excitement. Those who have it are born with it though, a susceptibility which had us labeled collectively as The Occularis, or 'The Eyes'.

Alice's was triggered by tensions at home, a series of heated arguments in a normally happy home. Mine, well I could only guess, but I think the general upheaval of abandoning my happy city life fit the bill. I had certainly got more than I bargained for and my entry into the Ocularis club did little to comfort me, a longed for answer seemed now depressingly hollow.

I closed my eyes and lay flat on my back, head throbbing from information overload when it hit me like a ton of bricks. I knew who could make sense of it all, the hospital, the gifts, but I had to find her first. At that point my exhaustion's full weight took effect and I felt sick with weariness, my limbs felt like lead and it took all I had to flick the light off and slump into my bed in my clothes. Naturally I didn't fall into a peaceful, gentle slumber. I tossed and turned; salient words from Alice's notes felt heavy in my mind as I tried to make sense of it all. It was too much.

HIDDEN

I smiled before I even looked as his hand swept into mine from behind me, the air around my fingers warmed by his proximity before the touch. It was like this world, me and Jake, school, was completely separate to the world I was in just last night in my room. This one was so much lighter and more hopeful and I pushed the rest out of my brain for just a few seconds to soak him up with all of my senses.

Talk. Sit. Work. Lunch, it all passed me by in a haze. Not a single thing, other than Jake had been able to take my mind off the inevitable. I knew exactly what I was supposed to do next but the logistics and potential for catastrophe seemed too daunting.

Taylor and Lydia seemed to have been engulfed by the cheerleading drama recently, so it was nice to see them in normal clothes. Taylor slumped into the chair next to me and rested her head on my shoulder with a pained sigh.

"Why so sad?" I mocked her with a pet lip. She broke a smirk and lifted her head into her hands.

"I'm totally bummed about not being here this weekend. I was so ready for our shopping and movie day but I have to go on grandparent duty with my parents so I'll be away all weekend."

Guilt stabbed me in the chest, I had been so consumed with my dark second life I had completely neglected to keep up to date with the two girls that made me feel normal. I would have definitely stood them up had this blip not saved the day.

I feigned sadness. "We can do it the weekend after Tay, it's no big deal." Lydia, uncharacteristically quiet laid a supportive hand on Taylor's wrist. "So where are you going, I mean where do your grandparents live again?" My eyes sought him out mid conversation like a child looks for a security blanket, locked on target I relaxed back into my conversation.

"Boston, well just outside, but I hate going there. They don't care if I go, I always get so bored and then everyone yells at me if I dare to plug in my IPod." Oh for her problems.

I had a date with Google and couldn't stay sitting around for long, but I had to make it seem like I was keen to listen to my friend's woes, I had done little to repay their kindness lately and if I wasn't careful I could find myself frozen out.

I made it through the rest of the day by turning my adrenaline into school work and glancing at Jake any chance I got, he was, without doubt the only thing keeping me sane.

As the bell heralded the end of the day students flocked out of the school gates like animals freed; swept along by the throbbing crowd I was out of the lot before I could even say goodbye to Lydia and Taylor. Jake thought I was going to help Mom, though I never actually said that I didn't correct him either. He had already been so accepting of my odd circumstances and behavior that I thought it best to leave him out of this bit, at least until I could figure out for myself what the hell everything meant.

My fingers moved with increased speed as my brain worked overdrive to pour out all the possible links and combinations in my mind. I decided working this out at home was safer, I didn't want to bump into anyone from school surrounded by all this witch crap, they already thought I was a weirdo, not that I could blame them for that.

Annie Stowell, Boston. The timer whirled for an eternity as I waited for the results. No, no, nothing, nothing. Then... 'Stowell's hospitality was outstanding and I would definitely recommend Adia Lodge to anyone seeking a great stay in a relaxing location.'

The name of the lodge was all I needed, the name of a lost friend backwards, I had found her. The review was a couple of years old so I dug a little deeper to be sure it was still going, it was. The address burned my palm as my grip tightened round it. I had to get there, soon. The logistics of getting there, paying for anything at all and getting my mom to believe some fabricated reason for an impromptu trip were insignificant in light of what I was possibly about to unearth. Then I knew, Taylor. I had somehow got to get in on her family trip. My body wracked with trepidation carried me to Jake's; I just needed a moment to feel safe.

I knocked quietly on the screen door, praying that the absent car meant I wasn't in for another dose of Dr. Mayer's kind of hospitality. Jake answered and I audibly exhaled. His face slipped into a smirk and he pulled me into the house, planting a thousand kisses on my face, rendering me helpless and only with it enough to inhale his scent.

"To what do I owe this honor Miss Roth?" He led me into the sitting room I had only glanced at in my rush to escape the Council meeting exodus last time. It really did look mainly normal, considering what an ass his dad was and how odd he always appeared. There was artwork on the walls that I hadn't noticed last time, just bland, nondescript oil paintings of dimly lit scenes. There were book shelves, the usual.

"Oh I don't know. Just needed to be around you for a while. It's ok that I just turned up right? I'm sorry, I should've called. Do you want me to go?"

He grabbed my shoulders playfully, "Scarlett, relax. I love that you came over. Now, make yourself comfortable and I'll get us a drink."

Jake passed through into the kitchen, leaving me to peruse the shelves. Must have been hundreds of books, lots of medical and legal books, made sense I suppose. The third shelf down didn't match really, full of books on the witch trials and Salem history, though half the town probably had that, just didn't seem like the kind of guy to go in for that, but, never judge a book by its cover. Seemed more relevant at this stage of my life than ever before. Perhaps they belonged to his mom anyway.

We sat talking, holding hands, it was amazing and exactly what I needed. If anything those moments made me more sure than ever that I needed to start taking control of my life and all the crazy webs of information I was finding. The sooner I knew what the hell I was dealing with, the sooner I could fix it, move on and start being a teenager again.

I felt like this was the first time we ever really got to be together, at least without him having to rescue me. It was physically painful to pull myself away but the light had dimmed and I was conscious that I had very little time to put my plan into place.

"Hey, before you go..." His arms pulled me back from the step into the house, and his arms. He must have read my mind.

"We haven't actually had a real date, not a normal one anyway. What do you say I pick you up later and take you out for a bit, do something fun?" That sounded like the perfect remedy for anything, but I needed so badly to start making progress at home and fix my life, but not one part of me was strong enough to resist the opportunity of time with him.

"Yeah, that sounds fun. I have some stuff I need to do so can you make it an hour or so?" Forgetting The Rules of new relationships I revealed my over excitedness too easily with a hurried little applause at the idea of an impromptu date. He laughed.

"You're such a dork!"

"Why, thanks. I guess I should be expecting something pretty damn special if that's how you think of me?" My face was wide with a smile and my cheeks ached.

"Well, I only have an hour, but let me see what I can do." With that he shoved me playfully onto the porch and shut the screen door. "See you in an hour Red." My dad used to call me that. A moment of total over the top relationship forecasting washed over me, and my head screamed how so many lifestyle features seemed to point out the man you were supposed to marry would often be like your dad. Jake. As a husband. I sighed without meaning too and just flashed him a smile laden with embarrassment as if somehow I thought he had heard my insane thoughts. That boy had no idea what he had let himself in for.

I yanked each side of my coat across myself until they overlapped and started to warm my chest. The air was particularly cold tonight and the inviting glow of lights from the houses on my way home made me pick up my pace. Mom was sat on the sofa when I got home and I realized that this was the first time I had seen her relaxing since we moved. She flicked her eyes up from the TV and motioned for me to sit with her; we used to always curl up under the same blanket when I was a kid, usually with a moutain of popcorn, salted for her and sweet for me, simple pleasures.

I allowed myself to switch off for a moment as I moved into the nook of her arm; she was warm and smelled of her perfume mixed with sweet things like fresh bread and cookies. I don't know what it was about moments like that but I felt five years old and just for a second as if nothing could touch me; though reality loitered in the corner of the room like a sinister shadow from childhood nightmares and it beckoned for me to leave my comfort cocoon behind.

Bearing in mind I hadn't progressed my plan at all it was a risk to ask Mom before I had even entertained how I would convince Taylor of my need to accompany her on a family vacation to Boston, but timing is everything with parents, another valuable childhood lesson, never forgotten.

"What's wrong sweetie?" She placed her hand on mine. "You look like you're about to ask me something. Is everything ok? Are you having troubles again?" I resented the use of the word troubles intensely and had to momentarily clench my jaw to avoid wasting my moment.

"Mom, seriously I'm fine. I was just thinking about something Taylor said at lunch today. She and her family are heading up to Boston at the weekend and she wanted to know if I could go with them?" I moved my gaze onto hers and drew a smile with my pleading expression.

"I don't see why not, but I am going to have to speak with her mom or dad, I can't just let you swan off with a family I don't know." I rolled my eyes and immediately wished I could take it back.

"Mom, come on! It's Taylor not some travelling freak show family." She tilted her head at me with just a look and I knew that as far as conditions went she would be sticking to it, it could have been worse though. "Ok, ok. I will have one of them call you once I have sorted the details." With that I hopped up, planting a kiss on her head before heading upstairs. Now just to sort out Taylor. I literally had no idea how that would work.

I logged onto to instant messenger, I was fairly confident I could track Taylor down that way. She spent half her life trying to join in on conversations with the older cheerleaders or Internet-stalking her latest fixation, not that I could really comment. I know where I would be spending all my time if I didn't have all this weird psychic power crap taking up space in my head. I didn't have much time, Jake was coming for me in less than half an hour and I still looked like the plainest version of myself.

SalemTay is online. I knew it.

Hey Tay…How's it going?

To me it all felt a bit obvious, like she would know I was only asking to move onto something else, but that's part of my problem, I am a chronic over-thinker on top of it all.

Yay. Don't normally find you here…all ok?

I was becoming more and more self-conscious that everyone seemed to automatically assume there was something wrong with me at all times, my cover wasn't working as much as I had hoped.

Yeah all good. I wanted to put a proposal to you actually, but I didn't want to put you on the spot in front of Lydia. I was thinking maybe you could do me a favor, but it's one that kind of benefits you, or I hope you'll think so…

OK shoot.

She was literally the fastest messenger I had ever known and Brooke was pretty impressive, I guess practice really does make perfect.

Well. It's a bit of a weird one. I've been doing my family tree, kind of a surprise for my mom for Christmas.

Here came that dark feeling again, my stomach tightened, I hated all this lying, but more how easily it was coming to me these days.

Anyway. I've found someone in Boston who I really want to speak to. She is one of the last living relatives on my mom's side and I think she can really help me piece things together, so I wondered if there was anyway your parents would let me come along. That way I can keep you company most of the time and I get to progress my project. Whaddya say? :)

The wait for a response felt like ages, I think mainly because I was so aware of the depth of my deceit and the guilt I felt for bringing yet another person into my ever more complicated life.

OMG!!! That is so cool and I love the idea. I'm going to speak to my parents tonight and we can plot tomorrow. This will be amazing. I'm totally staying up to create a road trip playlist.

I exhaled audibly, this was a good start. This may actually work.

Thanks so much sweetie. I know my mom will want to talk to yours if it gets the go ahead so try explain how important it is that she keeps what I'm trying to do a secret. Thanks so much, you're awesome!!

She posted a few more over excited messages before finally signing off and promising to go sort it all out with her parents. I got the impression that Taylor usually got her own way and if she had been whining so much about going I hoped her parents would see my tagging along as an easy route to keeping her quiet and occupied all weekend. I could see her now, all willowy limbs prancing into them and hassling them until they caved. I hadn't got to know her parents really, though chances were they had heard about me. No matter what your reputation, you can guarantee in a town like this one, that it has preceded you.

Right, makeover, quick. Hair down, always down, but combed through at least. Lip gloss on, flavored. Jeans, tight but not slutty and a floaty floral blouse, I would freeze but it surely it was his job to warm me up. I glanced at myself in the hall mirror and only noticed as I stepped away that it was hanging up now, Mom must have decided the limbo required to use it before was too much hassle.

Peering my head round the door I disclosed my plans with as little information as possible, not that I knew what I was doing anyway.

"Mom, I am going out with Jake for a while. I promise to be back by eleven. You don't mind do you?" I fluttered my eyelashes mockingly and she tried to wear her serious face.

"Scarlett. It's a school night, so make it ten thirty and keep your phone on please." She shooed me away with a look that screamed of 'go before I change my mind' and lifted the remote to flick channels. I was just having a final mirror check when I heard the car pull up in the drive.

"Bye Mom. Love you." I didn't hang round for the response; instead I skipped out the door before adopting a more casual stride as I moved into his view. He stayed in the car, hands firmly on the wheel. I slipped into the passenger seat and reveled in the way the car heater exaggerated his scent.

"Well hi. You look incredible." He squeezed my hand and left his own resting on my leg for a moment.

"Thanks, you smell incredible." He was smiling but my eyes were elsewhere, taking in his fitted plaid shirt and dark jeans, he was a god among men, well boys. Even his friends, with their football player physiques paled in comparison.

"So." Realizing I hadn't spoken in the longest time. "Where are you taking me?"

"Well, I hope you'll like it." With that he winked, and pulled out of the drive, guess I was supposed to wait to find out. Already eight pm, already I wanted longer with him and we had barely even started our date.

We drove past places I recognized and soon we were out of the zone I had committed to memory, there was still so much of this place I didn't know. We pulled up down a small side road, just past a pretty suburban street at what looked like a disused workshop and getting out of the car I could see that's exactly what it was. Slightly baffled I look to him and he smirked.

"Stop judging and trust me." He took my hand, placed his other over my eyes and plunged me into total darkness as he led me forward. The sound of the shop's wooden doors being unbolted made me jump and I heard him snigger. I felt him close the gap between us as he stole a swift kiss from my lips and they curled into a smile in its wake.

The door closed behind us and he moved his hands away as he stepped back to let me take it in. I didn't know what to say. Just a few feet inside, the concrete floor disappeared into a sea of throws, leading to two couches swathed in more fleecy blankets. Between them a small table laden with treats glistened below a web of thousands of twinkling lights. It was beautiful, romantic and so very me. I spun round and kissed him my thank you. The rest of the space was defunct bar a workbench and some old wooden drawers; but I was so swept up in the excitement it didn't matter.

Leading me over, he talked me through his little den. "So, I didn't know what you would like so I brought all sorts of stuff. We have savory... Chips, salsa, pitta, olives and we have sweet." My weakness amplified. Jake and a sugar rush combined was almost too much. He gestured to a fondue pot, full to the brim with melted chocolate, surrounded by cookies, marshmallows and slices of fruit.

"This is incredible, how did you do all this in an hour?" Needless to say, the perfection of it all had sent me into overdrive. I had no idea how I had managed this, but I knew I needed to work hard to stop him realizing he could trade me in for a cooler model.

"Well I use this place to chill out, it's my dad's." I experienced a momentary whack in the face with reality as the thought of his dad darkened my thoughts. "I actually did the lights and stuff a few days ago. I've been meaning to bring you here, but we just never found the right time. Anyway, sit, eat." His hand was in that magic spot in the small of my back and it was electrifying.

We took our positions, slouched on giant cushions either side of the table. We did the inevitable and went all Lady and the Tramp; feeding each other chocolate smothered marshmallows and trading stories about simple things. Turns out we did have more in common than an unhealthy fixation on one another. We liked the same music, bar my guilty pleasure pop collection which he deemed so tragic he couldn't even believe I would admit to it. I cried with laughter as he told me about all the stupid pranks he and Jason played on Tyler. We both had family in Florida, me a great aunt and him cousins. We joked about the chances we may have bumped into each other at a pool party one summer years ago and I liked the idea of him featuring in my past, my present and my future. It brought a security I longed for in such uncertain times.

Stuffed, we retreated to one of the couches where we lay knotted around each other, a mass of hormones and not so secretive longing. I glanced at my phone, almost ten. My heart dropped with what felt like an audible thud. How could it be going so fast? The oasis of calm that I had found in this evening was so needed and I felt sick at the thought of leaving this bubble to find myself alone in my room. Again.

I looked up at him and admired the shape of his jawline. "I need to be back by ten thirty." He shushed me with a finger across my lips and replaced it with his mouth. We kissed and kissed, what felt like years of hunger for him pouring out of me. I felt his reservation, his conscious decision to keep his hands on my back and he acted like a true gentlemen. I was disappointed but I knew he was right. We remained entwined until the very last moment; drawing out our time together as long as we could manage, but time had no regard for teenage lust and moved on regardless.

"Let's go. Come on. I want to stay in the good books and actually be allowed to take you out again." He punctuated his words with more kisses and dragged my reluctant body up from the embrace of the couch. "Come on; don't make this anymore... challenging. If I had my way we would just be locking ourselves in here." A wicked grin spread across his lips.

"OK. OK." I pouted, he ignored it and I lagged behind like a sulky child as we headed back to the car.

The ride back felt like a flight. I was high on chocolate; on him and I could smell him on my skin. Every time I moved my head the scent of him that lingered on my hair was disturbed and revitalized; it was intoxicating. We pulled up to the house and my stomach wrenched at the idea of retreating to my room, but I still had work to do and it was dangerous for me to be so close to him, wanting the way I did. He looked at me, sharing the longing and we made silent promises with some other worldly kisses before I forced myself to leave him there and head inside. It was almost a physical pain getting out of the car and I couldn't help but take one more look. He flashed me a smile and with that he sped off, taking all the comfort and new-found sense of relaxation with him.

With Jake gone I busied myself writing a to-do list for Boston in the back of an old journal. Pack what I needed, but pack light. Print off location map for the lodge. Take the notebook with me; I guessed I would need some kind of bargaining tool, if this information was so secret she wouldn't want to blow her cover immediately. I suppose she could always just tune into my thoughts to see why I was there, that would solve a few problems, and she'd have to believe me then.

My list turned into a page of 'don't forgets' and 'must takes' and it became hard not to feel some twisted sense of excitement. It was hard to describe, I didn't really know what I was doing, I suppose it all hung on the chance for me to be near someone like me, find out more about my powers and of course whatever happened in that hospital, I had become I inextricably linked into that too of course.

I spent the rest of that night reliving my time with Jake, the way his face was cast into shadow in the dim light and the way he had kissed me. My thoughts then turned to my trip, I saw the scene in my head, one was a helplessly romantic version in which my road trip led me to a world of answers that would set me free, the other dark and cold and served only to heighten my fears of what could be in store for me if my powers were left to evolve. I returned in my mind to the first journal, how my historical twin lost her love through one innocent touch passing a vision through to him and I shivered as my blood ran cold at the thought. Jake must not be brought into this, he must be protected. If I had learnt anything tonight it was that I was keeping him. I needed him.

By this point I was harboring so many notes on witches and powers and secret notebooks that I had started a collection in a box under my bed. It was a former shoe box, now a colorful montage of all the things in my life that mattered to me one particular day when I was fourteen. Pictures of boy bands and clothes I liked cut roughly from magazines and arranged in what had seemed an arty piece of self-expression. Some of the pictures were turning up at the ends now. It had been used to hide my secrets for years and it showed. I shoved it into the very middle, away from prying eyes and collapsed onto my bed phonc in hand. I wanted to text Jake, or better still get back round there but his dad would be in for sure by now and would not approve. I flicked through my contacts so the scroll bar reached top speed and bounced back to the top, Brooke's name stared at me from the screen. I had totally sucked since I moved. Almost involuntarily my legs swung off the bed and carried me back to the computer where I sat for an hour constructing more carefully written emails to her and to Dad. Not too chirpy so they would be suspicious, not too middle of the road so they would be worried, just the right amount of tedious gossip, it was like a Goldilocks tale for the 21st century. My calm alter-ego was playing an increasingly large role in my life; she was so much more normal than the real me in Salem.

Bed. Sleep. I was willing the morning to come round quicker for two reasons; Jake was picking me up and I would get to find out the verdict on my Boston trip plans.

UNDONE

Despite waking uncharacteristically early I found myself with very little time to get ready. I was working some kind of merged style at the minute, still finding the Salem me but it was working. Now there was Jake I felt totally obliged to make something of myself but in the most understated way. I opted for the outfit I had wanted to wear my first day but let my hair fall loosely the way he had suggested that time and gently patted a layer of gloss onto my lips before pulling on my book bag. This casual, yet glowing façade had taken me over forty five minutes to perfect.

Downstairs Mom was hurriedly searching for something, my guess was always keys, and she kissed me on the head as I passed her before sweeping the bunch from the hall table and whirling out the door, toast in mouth. She was the archetypal working mom, constantly juggling but somehow always managing to pull it off.

I was just bringing my coffee to my lips when I heard a car in the drive way. The speed at which I abandoned it caused a coffee tsunami to cover the table. "Crap!" I threw a towel over it and patted furiously before the idea that I might be wasting one second with Jake drew me away. I fled the kitchen like it was on fire, reaching the porch in record time to be greeted by the tantalizing outline of him. The fall sun behind him cast his features into dark shadow but I could feel him smiling. As he came fully into view he took my waist with his hands and kissed me furiously and with such passion it almost felt like a goodbye. Losing myself, I let myself slip into his arms as my bag slid to the floor. My back pressed up against the timber of the house and his frame shielded my eyes from the light, inside my stomach leapt and fluttered, his power over me was terrifying, magnetic and exciting all at once. I slid my face away from his, though it was against all my instincts and smiled.

"Good morning to you too." My hands, still on his face brushed his jawline and I felt the smile before I saw it; last night's lust was hanging thick in the air between us.

"Hi." He whispered, our faces still so close I felt the breath touch my cheek. "I have been thinking about that all night. Mm, better in real life." We let our hands find each other and headed to the car. He cast me several glances as he drove, each came with a slightly different smile and as ever in those seconds absolutely everything was ok. I couldn't help but fantasize that in a couple of weeks I may have some kind of future back, I could potentially have the answers I needed to at least control my powers, even if I couldn't get rid of them.

Our pairing was still grabbing attention despite the fact it had now been weeks, but the concern I used to feel when taking in their stares had become pride and I felt a little of my confidence spring to life.

I took the approach of one of his friends as a cue to leave and try getting hold of Taylor. It was cafeteria or gym hall for sure. I managed to make out the back of her head as I entered the food hall, she had Lydia with her who I could see was jigging excitedly so I feared the worst, that there was some breaking news in cheerleading land that I would have to endure. I had to admit to myself the possibility that maybe I was feeling a little left out, which was ridiculous, given that they had pleaded with me to join and I repeatedly shot them down.

"Oh my god Scarlett. It's going to literally be the best weekend of our lives." Lydia beamed as she stood up and squeezed the tops of my arms. I was confused for a moment, sensing it Taylor pulled Lydia back into her seat and offered some clarification.

"What loud mouth here means is I asked my parents if you could come along and they were totally cool with it and so I suggested as Adam is in Boston that Lyd might wanna go too, and as you can see, she's a little excited." Relief like I'd never known washed over me, this was a good day. Adam was Lydia's legendary and apparently hot-enough-to-die for brother, a source of much angst for her. She spent her life fearing her female friends were using her to get a chance to be near him. I didn't know what he looked like now, only in his grade school pictures but I could guess a male form of Lydia's heart-shaped face could live up to the hype, not that I cared, I had no interest in anything interrupting my plan or in other boys in general.

"That...my friends, is amazing!" We gave into our stereotypes letting out a high pitched scream in unison with little regard for our school mates or their eardrums. I could almost feel the tick in the theoretical friendship box from my outward display of excitement. If I had been a little distant and on the outside - I was back in for sure.

From that point the weekend arrived with relative speed. I told Jake about our trip and he was fine with it, though I was on orders to bring him something back by way of an apology for my abandonment. I felt an unease knowing how much distance there would be between us, fearful it might be far enough to erase what had become or even worse wake me from the dream of it all. He laughed out loud when I asked for one of his shirts to take with me so I could smell him while I was away, but he obliged and I took one long, drawn out breath as I packed my bag just so the memory of it was fresh in my mind.

Taylor's grandparent's house was like a museum, a perfectly preserved slice of the past complete with enough vintage clothing and paraphernalia to make an expert ebayer salivate. We spent the evening answering her grandma's questions, avoiding some questionable stew and playing card games we didn't understand before being excused to our room. We convinced the parents to let us all stay together and Lydia brought her laptop and the only film she ever watched; Sex and the City. The sleepover vibe was supported by a welcome stash of Reese's pieces, marshmallow fluff by the spoonful and a large bag of chips which we made embarrassingly light work of. We were are so happy and even I managed to bury my guilt about having an ulterior motive and join in.

It must have been four before we slept which translated into very bleary eyes at our seven o'clock wake up call. I splashed cold water liberally onto my face and locked eye contact with the me that stared back from the mirror, today was going to be a pivotal day in my young life. I could feel that, without any leaning towards positive or negative, I just knew today mattered. The familiar darkness I had become so accustomed too whirled in my gut and my hands tightened their grip on the cold porcelain wash basin. It was time.

Taylor's parents were remarkably laid back about my

intentions, though they gave me extra money and told me I had to take a taxi there and back, which I was glad about as it turned out I was ridiculously underprepared in more ways than one. They even called it and Taylor's dad came out to open the door for me; it was really sweet.

The cab joined the highway briefly and I opened the window to feel the rush of air on my skin. My palms grew clammy and the piece of paper I had scribbled the address on was softening under my vice grip. Anticipation burned my chest and cheeks and my stomach churned. I didn't even know if she would speak to me, or what I really wanted to know. I suppose just finding anyone connected to these notes was a start, she must be able to tell me something. By the time I had finishing thinking of all the varying scenarios that may unfold we were trundling through suburban Boston; with pristine houses stretching out ahead of us. The car pulled to a gentle stop and he flicked the keys in the ignition, bringing silence down on us.

"Here you are." He shuffled in his seat as he looked at me in the rear view mirror. I couldn't make out his accent, but his voice was soft and I didn't have that deep rooted fear with him I sometimes got in cabs; he wasn't the chop you up and lock you in a freezer type. He had a picture of what must be his wife and four kids strapped to the visor and I almost asked him to wait for me there, as security. I was deterred only by the fact I knew I couldn't afford it.

The journey had been shorter than I had anticipated, leaving me feeling tense. I suppose on some level I thought it would give me long enough to think of an opener because I still had nothing. I was shaking as I stepped out on the sidewalk with my destination reaching up in front of me.

The lodge was wooden, stained deep red with white windows; brightly colored curtains could be seen peering out from beyond the frames inside. Lifeless window boxes hung from each one, but it wasn't too hard to imagine them alive with color in the spring. Below the guesthouse signage a painted 'No Vacancies' sign swung from a post in the breeze and a black cat stalked over the path in front of me, causing me to hold my breath as I tried desperately to recount if that was bad or good luck. I chose to decide good and ignore the niggling feeling I was totally wrong.

I padded cautiously down the path and hovered at the door before reluctantly pressing the cold ceramic button on the ornate bell; the following seconds felt like an age. I smoothed my coat with my hands and pulled my bag into my side, placing a hand over the notebook's contour, it was my only link. I could hear the slow pace of approaching feet like a drum, getting closer to the door. The handled turned and a woman, about the right age stared at me. Her face was rosy, warm and framed by a soft bob of white hair. Her petite frame was smothered in a large sweater. It was cut in half by an apron covered in partial dusty hand prints that rested under her bosom.

I drew in a breath in preparing to say words I hadn't even decided on when she brought her hand sharply to her mouth. Before I could speak she slammed the door so hard I felt the air before my face rush past me. What the hell had just happened?

Against my better judgment I pushed the bell again. I heard nothing, not a single sound. I pressed my ear against the door, still nothing.

I crouched to the mail slot and pressed it open. "Hello? Ms. Stowell. I really need to talk to you. You don't know me, but I found something that might be of interest to you and I need your help. Please." I listened for a moment, I knew she was behind the door; I took a step back and watched as the handle slowly turned. A small crack appeared; her face largely shielded by shadows peered round. The warmth in her expression was replaced now by an indeterminable emotion, the closest I could get to it was blind panic or intense sadness.

When she finally spoke, it was just five words that powered my inner fears into total meltdown. "I know who you are." With that she pulled back the door and gestured for me to come inside. She didn't speak again for several minutes just pointed to a sitting room littered with mismatched but somehow complementary chairs. Had I been feeling more jovial I would have relished in its mad hatterness, but in sitting down I could only observe as she wrung her hands nervously and proceeded to pull them down her face with exasperation.

"I..." The words were trapped in my throat as if someone had sealed my mouth shut. I pulled my bag onto my knee and pulled out the little green notebook. I thought it might communicate my intentions more clearly. "What do you mean you know who I am?" Our eyes met for a brief moment before she looked down again, hers were swollen with tears that threatened to break out.

"I know who you are. She told me you'd come," she was almost whispering as her voice failed to hide the strain. "I didn't know when but I knew you would, her visions were always accurate. And forgive me, but I have been praying for decades that this time she was wrong. I wanted an end to this." She wiped her eyes with a crumpled tissue from her apron pocket and I shifted uncomfortably in my seat. She made no additional effort to speak; preferring instead to avoid looking at me as if she hoped the awkward air would be too much and I may just give up and leave. She clearly did know how badly I wanted some answers.

"I found this in my local library. Hidden or just abandoned." I extended my arm and lay the notebook gently in her lap. "Alice left it for someone to find. I need your help to understand what I am meant to do with it. It has a personal relevance to me as well so it's really important I understand what she wanted it to mean. To be used for."

She raised a hand the way a school mistress might to silence a class and shook her head violently as if ridding herself of some invisible torment. "You have no idea what you are getting yourself into, none at all. You should leave now and destroy this, forget you ever saw it." She raised her voice and my cheeks flushed with embarrassment and fear.

"I can't. I have these…"

"Visions I know. Alice saw this whole thing. She didn't leave that book by chance, it was meant for you. Don't you see? Alice's powers were strong; she had the most developed foresight I have ever known. This stuff is dangerous. She was wrong to say a thing about what happened there; it's not worth what happened to her or what would happen to you and me if this ever got out. You need to leave, now." She stood up, the woman who I saw when she first answered the door was gone, this version of her was as defensive as a lioness, and she meant every word.

"Please. I need to understand what happened, to stop it happening again, that's what she wanted." I paused, but realized there was no real point in holding back now. "And I'll be honest. I want to know if you can help me stop my visions or at least control them. You must know something; you can't be around people like Alice and Aida and not learn anything about it. Though I guess you could probably hear in my thoughts that that's what I wanted to know." My voice pleading; I stared at her face, willing her to acknowledge that she could do something, anything. I was not leaving even more confused than I came.

"I don't do that anymore. I learned to block it out after we escaped. It was suffocating me." She moved from her standing position in to the seat alongside me and in a move that totally shocked me, placed her warm hand over mine. Her eyes locked right on mine for the first time since I arrived.

"Scarlett. There are darker forces at work here than I doubt you have ever imagined. This isn't a campfire ghost story; it's a real-life nightmare that you are asking me to lead you into. Sometimes we need to stop trying to find answers and just live. I am old now and I have lost so much of my life, almost all of it on this. Your best chance to lead a normal life is to go home to your parents and be a kid. This is not the world for you." Her face had softened, she squeezed my hand.

"I appreciate your concern for me, I do, but I am too involved now and finding Alice's notebook just made it worse. If you don't help me I won't stop searching until I find someone that will, but I would much rather it was you. Please?"

She bit her lip and shook her head in silence. She walked over to a large oak dresser which displayed more mismatched stuff, polka dot plates alongside fine china decorated with delicate flowers and the kind of plastic water jugs you saw at kids' parties. With her back to me I could only hear the shuffling of paper and items thudding against the inside of drawers as she searched for some mystery object.

She placed an envelope next to me. "She told me when you came asking questions I had to give you this. I have carried it around so long. It's why I had to go; she would talk constantly about this red haired girl called Scarlett. You were in a recurring vision she had. It got so bad she would wake up screaming your name." She brought he hands over her eyes as if shielded herself from the memory. "When she told me she saw them coming for her years down the line I said I couldn't take anymore, I didn't want to know my future. She made me take this and promise to hold on to it, that you would come and I couldn't bring myself to break that promise."

She shunted the envelope forward; I took it in my hands, rubbing my fingertips over my name on the front. It was an eerie experience to know this had been waiting for me for over forty years. I slid my fingernail under the edge of the opening but it was abruptly interrupted with a firm hand.

"No. Not here. I will tell you what I can but I do not want to know the extent of what is in there, you must take it away with you. That is your story, not mine." With that she switched into hostess mode and cheerfully went off to make a pot of coffee, adding something about biscuits as she pottered and padded around in the next room, her slippers shuffling as she walked.

I took in my surroundings; her penchant for thrift-store chic was impressive and there was something hugely cool about the off-the-wall décor and homeliness she had created. I turned to the small telephone table alongside my seat which housed a retro lamp made of yellow blown glass and a small silver cat. I reached out a hand to pick it up; intrigued to see if it was real silver and while my hand was maybe an inch away I blinked and found I was holding it. Eyes closed, open again and it hadn't moved at all. My heart rate spiked, as it seemed to be doing almost daily - my hand was still waiting there. If it wasn't that I was already weary with new found freakishness I would have sworn it moved into my grasp. I shook off the notion and instead chose to acknowledge I was insane.

When she came back the room was engulfed by the aroma of freshly ground coffee. A silver rimmed cream jug sat next to a surprisingly coordinated sugar bowl on an antique tray. This felt odd and while I was pleased I seemed to have her more on side, it did not bring me the peace of mind I had envisaged. It was like we were playing house, painting on pretend smiles all the while my curiosity and her lack of it fought silently between us.

I stirred my coffee again and again unable to draw my mind away from the spot on my thigh where the small envelope rested moments before, it left a burning imprint as intense as my desire to rip it open and devour the secrets it held.

We spoke in hushed voices; there were obviously paying guests in the house and I didn't blame her for not wanting to air this information in public.

Rather bizarrely, we exchanged pleasantries for a while; she told me about the lodge, how she had used it as a focus for her attentions to get over what had happened to Aida and her painful separation from Alice, she even took me on a tour. It was a beautiful old house and her eye for quirky color schemes and collectables had created a haven of homely calm. A total paradox to the world we were soon to venture into.

She shared her experiences at Danvers to an extent, but I could sense she was holding back. At one point she broke off mid-sentence as a young, amorous couple emerged from their room giggling and kissing. They were oblivious to us on the landing and both Annie and I stood fixated on them until the front door closed behind them; both of us most likely wishing for our own opportunity to walk care free into the outside world.

The moment passed and she re-entered her account of which even the edited version sounded like something from Frankenstein; frontal lobotomies, operations with little or no anesthesia, food rationing and there was the parts I knew about most of the patients not even being sick.

"But I need to know what you know about why it was happening." I knew she had been avoiding this part and that it probably had a little more to do with what was in my envelope than she was comfortable with.

"Alice said we all there at the hands of Sutcliffe because he was obsessed with the supernatural. Apparently he was paying the authorities to keep quiet so he could study, in any way he saw fit, cases where people exhibited special symptoms."

"Powers?" She nodded. "As time went on, we lost friends as you know and Alice's visions became stronger and stronger. She couldn't sleep and sometimes they were so severe she would collapse into convulsions. She had a complex theory, well explanation about why he was doing it but I really don't want to say it out loud. You will find everything you want to know in that envelope. But Scarlett. I am warning you. Once you have read it, it cannot be undone and knowing that information will make you vulnerable. So take it with you and if you can bear it, please take at least a day or two to decide if it is really worth knowing. There is still a chance for you to experience the world as it was meant, but only if you leave all this behind, now." What an odd thing to say.

Once again she placed a hand on mine and forced my eyes upwards with her stare. "Promise me?" I nodded and stood up from my seat. I spontaneously threw my arms round her and held her in a real goodbye, I knew I wasn't coming back but I felt a genuine bond with her through Alice and I was so grateful she had let me in. The rest was up to me.

I glanced at my watch, it was almost four, I had been gone five hours nearly, and it was time to get back. My cab arrived and we exchanged another silent hug. I watched her watching me leave and wanted desperately to know what she was thinking now and if she knew what my decision would be, because after that encounter and seeing the fear in her eyes, I didn't know myself. The truth had become marginally less appealing.

I spent the journey back pulling the envelope out of my bag and then thrusting it back in. I must have turned it over to open it a hundred times but it didn't seem like the right time or place, besides, I had little time before I would be back with Taylor and Lydia and I had to bury my angst in favor of a sunnier disposition.

My new found talent for fabricating significant sections of my life came in handy round the table when conversation turned to me and my day of genealogy research. Guilt weighed on my chest as I stared at the happy, attentive faces soaking up my lies. Two of them my only friends in Salem. A wave of nauseous heat surged up my body and I excused myself for an early night. Looking at them was too much and the secrets waiting for me upstairs were whispering to me, a call so strong it was almost animal, like a predator drawn to its prey.

Unfortunately though, I feared I was the prey in this darkening scenario.

With some brief time alone I retrieved the envelope from its hiding place in the base of my weekend bag; a small tear in the lining was just accommodating enough to keep my burden safe from prying eyes. I made little progress, an hour passed and I was still cross-legged on the floor hoping for the courage I needed to open the envelope. The paper felt warm from my touch; the writing on the front was wearing slightly from my constant tracing of the lettering with my index finger. The room was silent apart from the occasional muffled sound from downstairs as the rest of the party laughed and joked in front of a lit fire.

"Alice. I'm scared. I don't know what to do." I had always thought I was slightly odd for talking to myself, but talking to dead people was a new low for me. I didn't know what I was going to do with this information, whatever it was, but the emotional and physical reaction I was having to its proximity told me I wasn't ready to open it, and somehow being away from home made it worse. That was the first time I had ever called Salem that.

It was dusk by the time Taylor's car pulled into our driveway and the evening light filtered through the neighboring trees to create long, winding shadows like trip wires in my path. The journey had been awash with talk about Lydia's reunion with her brother and I somehow managed to duck out of answering any further questions about my own Boston adventures.

I waved them off with a convincing smile which proceeded to fade the second they went out of view. My hands ached from holding onto my bag but the weight of my clothes was nothing compared to the feeling of carrying the envelope so I was both surprised and happy to find the door unlocked when I got back, it meant Mom was in the house. I peered round the dining room door, she wasn't there but I learned to track Mom as if I were some ranger and she the bear. There were traces of recent activity, a coffee mug, which when brushed with a hand was still radiating heat. Next to it a plate with some remains of a bagel and her phone, so she wasn't far.

She gave herself away clinking cutlery around in the drawer; spinning on my heels I followed the sound into the kitchen. Mom stared up from an open jar or peanut butter and jelly, her spoon wielding hand poised midair. She smirked and let out a belly laugh that infected me from across the room. She reached back into the open drawer and passed me a spoon. Carefree for a moment I grabbed it and we indulged in unison

"So", she paused while she tried to remove the gum like paste from the roof of her mouth. "How was Boston? Did you have a great time with Taylor and her family?" There is was again, guilt. I swallowed it down, deep into the pit of my stomach where I kept all the dark, unpleasant feelings I had been having lately.

"Oh, it was so awesome. Her grandma is this amazing old woman, and the house, you should have seen it, so crazy. I seriously think she must have had every kind of knick knack available to man." My attempt at high speed conversation Lydia style had baffled Mom into submission.

"That's so great honey. I think you needed a break. It's all been pretty full on since we moved." With that and her clear but covert acknowledgement of the results of my visions, I managed to break away and needing to talk to Jake was the perfect excuse. Nothing said normal teenage girl more than a growing infatuation with a boy. Mom grinned and shooed me away with her fingertips.

I really did want to speak to Jake, but I wasn't sure I could hold that conversation; there was only so much I could take at once. I tossed my bag onto the floor and reached into the inside pocket of my coat where it now waited for me to retrieve it. It was alive with intrigue and history. Just holding it in my fingers sent a tingle of fear laden anticipation up my arm to the nape of my neck. It always happened like that; in situations of extreme distress or excitement I got this strange feeling, almost a tingle, but more like my neck was suddenly hollow and filled with a rush of cool air. I could never describe it exactly right, the one time I tried Brooke said I was crazy, but my body was dead on this time, I had never been more complicatedly lodged between the two emotions.

My breathing was audibly quicker, and the extra effort being made by my heart pushed my chest outwards rhythmically. Whatever Alice knew, not just about the hospital, but apparently me, was in my hands and the burden was more intense than I could have imagined. People always joke about whether or not they would like to know their fate, so easy to talk about it but so few are ever faced with it.

I braced myself. Shuffling backwards I propped myself straight up against my bed head. Crossed legged I slid my shaking index finger in the only gap of the envelope's seal. I paused, exhaled and began running my finger between the two sides of paper, the space widening on the envelope giving me a sneak peak at the paper inside. It was open. Confusion was the first feeling that hit me. Without touching the contents I could see three folded pieces of paper and a hint of wax on one of them.

I pulled the contents onto my bed. Three individual letters, each sealed and numbered. I hadn't been prepared for a trilogy. I placed two and three back in their paper hiding place and rested it on my nightstand. Number one stared at me defiantly, teasing me with ghostly outlines of words on the reverse of the paper, their illegibility made me hungry to tear it open.

Dear Scarlett, The fact that you are reading this fills me with such mixed emotions. I am glad you have managed to find the information I left you and used your ingenuity to put the pieces if this bizarre jigsaw together, though I suppose that was inevitable, it confirms all I feel I know about you and shows I have been right about you all this time. But, I am also saddened, saddened that you are thrust into this world, one in which you are about to discover you are the prey.

I felt sick. Even without a vision I could see what was about to unfold, though I clung with every shard of my being to the hope that it was as far-fetched as it seemed.

I know you have read many things about women like us, and I know what you seek more than anything is answers, a way to make them stop. I cannot promise you that. My purpose is to warn you, prepare you in any way I can for what I know is coming. I have been having visions about you for some time, mainly since I left Danvers, but some before...once they started they came more and more frequently with ferocious clarity.

I have written this letter in stages to try and let you keep some sense of control; I more than anyone know how powerless you feel in these early days. That said, I cannot afford to mince my words; your life is at risk.

Sutcliffe, the doctor I told you about in my previous communication is part of a group that has been tracking our kind for years. He was 'collecting' girls for the hospital in order to to remove them from society, but also so he could experiment on them. He believed we were an abomination and abused his position of power to act out his sick fantasies in a bid to create a purer world, he wasn't alone.

He was part of an ancient movement, a secret society that has been persecuting us since the start of civilization. Their heyday was the witch trials. Turning us into a brand gave them all the ammunition they needed to commence years of unlawful killing, exile and worse. We are the hunted and from the moment you had your first vision you became a target.

In today's society's eyes witches largely only exist in fiction and you and I would certainly not conform to that label, outcasts or eccentrics maybe, but to these vile creatures we are to be exterminated like vermin. They believe us to be a curse, a blemish in society and will stop at no lengths to capture, kill and punish us. To them we are witches and they wish to end our kind in the kinds of ways I know you are familiar with, but society has evolved, and they have been forced to amend their tactics, tailoring them to allow them to operate without challenge in an ever more accepting and diverse society.

Their name is The Venari. Members are everywhere, but they are meticulously careful not to be exposed and they are the reason I am not able to pass this information on in person. From the moment we escaped a hunt began to track and kill us, they feared our combined gifts were making them vulnerable. Annie is not free, they know where she is and they are watching very closely, but her unwillingness to speak of her experiences and decision to abandon her gift has bought her some time, though not much, that is another story.

I have seen them focusing on you, gathering their evidence and trying to work out if you have the gift. They are closing in but I cannot see every detail. That is the purpose of my letters, to give you what I know to aid you in the fight.

The next two letters contain more details on the things I have seen, but there is so much to say and so much to take in. I will sign this off now and hope you can forgive me for laying this burden on you. I must say now...I do not know how this story ends, so don't rush to read on for that reason; you must only do so if you are ready to see what is inside them. I believe in you.

Alice x

My hands were shaking and something swelled within my gut that I couldn't explain. Fear seemed like such a small and insignificant word for the enormity of the sensation. Was this what real terror felt like? A harrowing darkness turned and flexed in my belly and my eyes stared at the two remaining envelopes. She didn't know how my story ends, she said that, so there was no reason to run away with the idea that my life would soon be over, but I couldn't deny that it what it felt like. A real, looming threat.

I took a minute, paralyzed by a hideous feeling of emotional and mental exhaustion to compare in my mind the differences between my life in Washington just a couple of months ago and this; sitting in my room discovering that my entire existence was known to people years before I was even born, that I was now classed a witch and that this information could make me cease to be. How could this happen?

I didn't understand what this meant. Ok, so my visions make me vulnerable, well ok, I hadn't had one for a while so maybe they were over, then what? I felt a dip, like I was on a ride that was making that tiny last shift into free fall. I had to find out more, but it wasn't going to be tonight. I needed to try and rest, though the very idea of sleep was about as realistic as me waking up in Washington tomorrow and this all being the most ridiculous, cruel dream.

I picked up my phone; I needed to hear his voice. It had proved itself to be the only thing that calmed me here. My fingers could barely hit the keys, my eyes bleary from unexpected tears; the two rings it took him to answer were too long.

"Well hi. I was wondering when you would be back." He was so excited to speak to me, I could tell and usually that would have sent me soaring but not tonight.

"Hi. Yeah sorry I've been back a couple of hours, but just been sorting through my things you know." Just tell him, tell him everything before it eats you alive. My mind was pushing and pushing but I wasn't ready for that, I couldn't risk driving him away, I was too close to the proverbial edge to risk losing him.

"You ok, you don't sound so pleased to be back?" He was concerned, if only he knew. Before I could answer he started to speak again, preventing the potential word vomit from escaping my mouth. I lost myself in the conversation, not in its content but the mere sound of his voice. The short, sweet intakes of breath between sentences revived me, each one offering a tiny amount of hope. I could and would face whatever was coming for me, if for no other reason than the almost primal desire I had to be near, kiss, and touch him.

"If you think you can get out, my dad is out tomorrow, some council meeting but another member is holding it, they have a special guest or something." I could tell he was smiling and the idea of time, alone, with Jake was the perfect, if not only antidote right now.

"Are you kidding? My mom works so much I could probably stay over and she wouldn't notice." Wow, smooth. Just invite yourself to stay over. Idiot. "God, I didn't mean I should stay I just meant it will be fine."

With an audible smile he graciously overlooked my comment and we made our plans. In that moment I decided. Despite everything I had said and thought up to now, I was going to tell him all about Alice, the secret society, every detail. If he freaked out and couldn't handle it at least I would know now before it went too far.

I drew myself a bath, a place to lie whilst I considered my fate. The call of envelope number two was deafening, a constant, progressive percussion resounding through my head and chest. The clear water left a molten ring of heat around my ankles and I had no choice but to pause to acclimatize. I caught a glimpse of my disheveled reflection; hair lank and streaked with anxious sweat and oil clung to my head and served only to accentuate the newly acquired bags of grey, mottled skin below my eyes.

The macabre fanfare emanating from the envelope acted as a dark lullaby that sang me into a shallow and troubled sleep. Lurid dreams merged into one as the night passed in a flash of cold sweats and shallow, nervous breaths.

School had never taken longer to be over than that day. I had more than worn out my fake pleasantries. It seemed an eternity since I opened the first envelope and even longer since I moved here. My life had become so disjointed from my old world that I could barely trace the lines of my dad's face in my mind, or hear Brooke's laugh. I went back to the library; I suppose to find some familiar comfort in books but this situation tested even that.

I went through it in my head. Witch Trials. Salem. Danvers. Danvers. Danvers. That one specific word replayed in my mind over and over. I knew it, or had seen it somewhere before. I mounted a separate search and there it was. It wasn't just the name of the hospital; it was one of the most recognizable names of places caught up in the hysteria of the Witch Trials. Witches were examined there and even now it housed a memorial to the victims, as a reminder for us to be tolerant. Seemed some people needed a refresher on that. It seemed so obvious now that they would poke fun at our ignorance and naivety by returning to the scene of the crime. Re-committing them in ever more creative ways right there, just centuries later. Yet, it was somehow clumsy and arrogant, were they so sure they had been careful enough never to be caught? Perhaps. But, here I was – knowing. Admittedly, I had help. Couldn't someone else have figured it out too? Then the realization that, yes, others may have tried to extinguish their reign of megalomania, but if they had; they hadn't survived. I gulped down the palpable fear of what this could mean for me and my head bowed under the invisible, but immense pressure of it.

To say it was surreal was the biggest understatement ever. I felt like a child; a ball of nervous energy crouched under a comforter listening to a scary story. This kind of stuff was for fairy tales and horror stories; bad guys and witches and secret societies - not real life. Not my life.

My paranoia kicked into overdrive too. I examined the faces of the people around me - Tall, Dark-Eyes guy was nervously glancing from side to side. What was he up to? Probably nothing more than trying to conceal his huge selection of romantic fiction. Then there was Grungy, Skater Girl. She was writing angrily in a worn notebook; perhaps doing the same as me. Our eyes accidentally met and I felt myself flush as I desperately sought a new focus. Literally anyone could be in on this, it was terrifying. I nervously scooped up my things and headed for the odd sanctuary of the house.

The weight of my situation made the gap between normality and where I found myself now, widen with every passing moment and as I stood on the bridge, taking in the river and the light dancing through the trees beyond, my hands began to tighten around the wood involuntarily. A familiar, unwelcome wooziness surged through my already buckling frame and I felt my face hit the boards where my feet had been only moments before. Then it was black. I knew this was one of them, a vision, and from deep within my paralysed state I willed it to be over, there was no hint of curiosity. There was nothing this could show me that I would want to see.

The black faded and the confused pixels of my vision began to meet up to form a picture. Through my eyes, this one was through my eyes. I was watching, my own hands, hearing my heart beating. I felt a large, warm bead of sweat as it gathered pace and raced from my clammy forehead to my chin. Tremors rocked my arms and my hands danced awkwardly at the ends of my wrist trying to grasp a piece of paper. It wasn't clear, I couldn't see the words, I wasn't able to figure out if it was my eyes in the vision or my mind now, cold from its hard landing place that was malfunctioning at this most frustrating of moments. The vision me was finding it hard to catch her breath and I was mimicking the motions unintentionally.

I had seen this place before; I recognized the smell of cold concrete and paper. I couldn't place it. Then my memory sprang to life revealing the mystery in part, Jake's dad's garage. Still my eyes refused to identify what it was that was causing future me to feel such intense emotions. It wasn't to be and before I could absorb the words on the paper my eyes reverted to their cold, horizontal perspective and I lay on the cold ground for a few moments before I was able to force myself inside.

I stood and examined my reflection like I had that first day; so much had changed and yet so little of it was visible. In my mind though; I was a different person. I knew of darkness that I hadn't ever comprehended before and things, about me that seemed impossible. The mirror, still not hung, was now surrounded by scrawled paint samples; childish daubed lines of Mom's attempts to create a home, but in the wake of a fresh vision my growing sense of comfort was obliterated.

It was time to go to Jake's and I had managed to bring a touch of color back to my face; seeing him was a tantalizing prospect even in the circumstances. I assumed some semblance of normality by fixing my hair, changing my clothes – which had been stained with the winter dirt. I patted on the faintest hint of rose balm, praying silently that he got to taste my efforts that evening.

Keys and car at my disposal I decided to drive, the air was bitter, the roads dark and my recent vulnerability haunted me into the safer option. I channeled my nervous energy into getting there quickly and within seconds I found myself waiting for the safety of his shape to appear the doorway.

He stared at me so intently it bordered making me nervous. "You look amazing." At the same time as his words hit my ears his hands wound into mine and he led me into the front room.

"Thanks. I hardly think jeans and a t-shirt constitute amazing but hey, I'm happy if you're happy." We both smiled widely and landed as a heap of person, each indistinguishable from the other. My mind was a jumble of conflicting thoughts, some simply focused on inhaling him and enjoying these moments, the others on how do I tell him? What do I tell him, and how can I get some time alone to find out what the hell was on that paper?

Moments later, Jake appeared in the doorway clutching a handful of takeaway menus and I felt a pang of guilt for not even noticing his absence. He slumped back into the Jake shaped dent in the couch beside me and thrust the glossy papers in my face.

"So, lovely lady." His face wide in that smile I knew was just for me. "What do you fancy? My treat." His hands, manly beyond his years were fanning out the options as if he were a croupier offering a winning hand. I followed the shape of his hands right up his arm and to his jaw, where something instinctive took over and I found myself suddenly on him, legs straddling his frame, his face in my hands and lips pressed furiously against his. His momentary surprise was soon replaced with a passionate reciprocation and his kissed mouth burst into a wide smile which caused a burst of burning self-consciousness to spread and I retreated to my seat.

"Hey. Where'd you go?" He feigned a pet lip and brushed my now grown out bangs to the side, revealing my embarrassed eyes. "I was enjoying that, you." I smiled and changed the subject back to food.

"I say pizza, from that little place on Trewent Boulevard." I pushed the menus aside and patted his leg playfully. I knew that place didn't deliver, Mom and I ordered from there a couple of days after we moved and it was average, but this way Jake would have to go fetch it and I would have at least half an hour to dig around. Guilt, guilt, guilt.

"Fine, as it's you. I'll go to the one pizza place in this stupid town that is collection only." He launched himself up with a thrust of power from his arms and tossed his car keys in the air before catching them with a clink. "Must be love." And with that he turned on his heels and walked out, leaving me in a state of confused bliss, grinning and stirring over in my mind. I knew it wasn't the same as saying he loved me directly but, hey, this was Jake Mayer, I'd take that.

I realized I had to move, fast. My mind now focused on the task at hand. I moved cautiously and quickly through the illuminated house, feeling like an amateur thief. The door to the garage fortuitously unlocked meant I didn't have to rifle nervously through the keys I had taken from the hook as I sloped through the kitchen where he had held me that day. The compulsion to look over my shoulder was immense but I had to get on, I couldn't let Jake find me here, so I turned the lights off and operated by phone light.

Being in that garage was like entering my own mind, seeing what I saw and smelling what I had smelt was so bizarre. The table, previously populated by Mayer senior and his equally uptight friends lay barren and unlit, I flicked the switch to improve my chances but it sent white hot fear coursing through my veins, he could come back early, that would be worse than Jake finding me here.

The only place there could be anything was a solitary filing cabinet in the left hand corner, it had been out of view from my window hiding spot, but inside it was the only focal point. I crouched down before it, hands trembling and breathing fast and erratic. There was a padlock holding the clasp shut and I panicked. I had nothing to open it. I grasped frantically at the single hair grip in my hair, pinning one side of my hair off my face and in a true movie moment began prodding away at the lock. To my complete shock it sprung open with a click, and I realized I had almost been hoping it would be the get out clause I needed, that I would have had to abandon my task and wait like a normal girlfriend, in the warm house flicking through the endless boring TV channels.

I laid it down beside me and slid the first of two drawers open. Alphabetized files, the kind you see in offices everywhere filled it. I started pulling them forward, without any idea what I was looking for. Without thinking I slammed the top drawer shut and moved to the second. My fingers working independently, knowing where they we going before I could recognise it myself. M, m. I was saying the letter out loud. I found the section and then I saw it, in plain sight and found myself living the vision I had from earlier that day.

Alice Markham. Then her life told in a handful of cold, hard words. Identified. Incarcerated. Escaped. Tracked. Captured. Then the word I knew was coming, DECEASED. This was a log sheet, her existence reduced to a few lines in a lonely filing cabinet. The document was signed, five names, I processed them one by one, the last one causing my heart's race to step up a gear, Clayton

Mayer. The paper was branded with a crest, the kind you find on stationery at some fancy country club; swirling plumage or foliage encircling the central character, V.

I psychically felt the click in my mind. Venari, the secret society in Alice's letters, the feeling I always had around him and the secret meetings. My mind whirled and the sweat charted its predetermined path down my face onto my chin. I remained aware of the lack of time, despite my fear, confusion and panic. I aggressively folded the paper so it would fit into my jeans pocket, slammed the drawer shut and replaced the lock at speed. Escaping as silently and as carefully as I came in I took my position when he had left me and just in time. The engine of Jake's car roared to a stop in the drive almost simultaneously to the moment I flicked the TV on. I didn't know how to begin to process what I had found, or how to pretend I hadn't. I was threatened by silence or the curse of offloading the most complicated and terrifying series of events to the boy I, well, the boy I loved. How do you address your boyfriend with questions about his potentially mass murdering, intolerant, secret society participant father? It's far from standard date night talk.

My hands twisted and turned within each other and I could still feel the damn sweat as Jake breezed through, and carefree, planted a kiss on my head. Straight into the kitchen he clattered cutlery and glasses before emerging with pizza on plates, an obvious bid to impress me as I knew no teenage boy in the world would create unnecessary washing up. My heart pounded and I was painfully aware I hadn't spoken or made eye contact with him since he walked in.

UNVEILED

I pushed food around my plate while Jake chatted; blissfully unaware of what was coming. In my head I worked through all of the ways I could broach a subject like this. The usual warmth and safety I felt from his presence replaced by fear and a kind of loss, nothing could be the same.

Words began forming in my mouth, hot on my tongue like fire. "Jake. I need to talk to you about something." I looked down, weighed by the burning desire to take the words back instantly. He froze mid bite and promptly put his slice down, brushing his hands together before switching his position to face me.

"Mm. Ok, shoot." Even now he hadn't sensed the fear, he was so ready for me to start making Christmas vacation plans or start dropping hints about presents. I loved Christmas, for me, until this year, the run up to the holidays was the best time of the year, still so magical and warming. I lived those weeks, each year like a movie, buzzing with real joy at all the comings and goings, trimmings and the way people became a little more together even if only for a while. Mom, Dad and I always still spent Christmas together even since the divorce. Dad would stay in one of the spare rooms so we could still have Christmas morning together, and he would make a tower of his special festive pancakes, which were only separated from the standard kind with a sprig of fake holly that sat longing for use the other three hundred and sixty four days of the year.

"I have had a couple more visions, since the dance." Pausing, scratching around in my mind for the right words I couldn't hold his gaze. He placed a reassuring hand over mine to stop their twitches and with a careful index finger, lifted my chin away from my chest before leaning over to me and placing the gentlest, most loving of kisses on my lips. I wanted to savor that taste, that sensation; I didn't need foresight to know this could be the last I got from him.

I grabbed the hair at the back of his neck, pushing his mouth against mine and letting him part my lips with gentle searches of his tongue. I let the kiss evolve into its beautiful, satisfying conclusion, though the hunger it brought me was unsettling and I sensed his longing, the space between us filled with palpable craving. Our heads resting together with the slightest touch of our foreheads, air from warm, desperate mouths met between us and the selfishness within me to let our closeness play out won me over, the concerns and mass of frightened words I was preparing to say retreated to the darkness of my mind, now full only of images of us now, then, in the future. There were some experiences I wasn't willing to miss out on, and this, with Jake was one of them.

Still so close, his hands filled with my hair as he cradled my head his mouth spoke and his sweet breath washed over my face bringing with it the warmth that had been stolen just a matter of minutes before. Being with him was like starting again, he could make it all better.

"You drive me so crazy Scarlett." He exhaled a breath as much tormented as filled with pleasure.

"It's hard to be a gentleman with you here on my couch, looking so." He shook his head playfully. "So appealing." He moved away, I think for fear he was breaking some code by saying the words. His body shifted away, back to his original position. So consumed with teenage lust he had already forgotten my solemn declaration, promising a serious talk and was too distracted even to eat.

"You are always a gentlemen Jake, but I'm not a china doll, you won't break me you know." I slid a hand along his thigh and pulled myself to sit over him. He let out an audible groan.

"I want what you want." My lips found him and

without speaking again we found ourselves tangled together, a mass of hormones and deep, excitable breaths. I watched, with awe as he pulled his t-shirt over his head in a fluid, intoxicating movement and I felt myself stir with a kind of anticipation I had never known before. My failed attempt to have the talk was threatening to push its way into my mind but I wouldn't let it take this from me. If my days were numbered this was more important than ever.

He placed soft kisses along the side of my torso and we were lost together, miles away from the torment of real life. Here there was only longing and the satisfaction that came with getting the thing you wanted most in the world.

Later as we lay dozing, Jake's hand brushed my shoulder as my face carved a home in the nook of his shoulder and chin. I sensed he was going to speak way before he made any noise, I felt the rumble of his pulse quicken.

"I love you Scarlett Roth." He said nothing else, he didn't have to. I wanted to say it back without a gap, immediately, but I realized that was too eager, though I had little time for games. I looked up at that face, the one that had saved me so many times, even without realizing and said the most natural and real thing in the world.

"Good. Because I love you too." That felt so good to say.

"We better get ourselves together; my dad could be back soon." Those simple words dragged me abruptly from my euphoria to the world, the one I lived in which was growing increasingly sinister by the day. Knowing what I knew made it even more terrifying to think of seeing his father. Jake was sighing intermittently and couldn't refrain from touching me, his hands stroking the length of my outstretched arms. In another time, everything would have been the most perfect it could ever have been. If I could have transported us into a secluded lodge or a tropical beach my life would have been complete. Not true, it was complete with him. The cruel twisted hands of fate had surprised even the pessimist I was becoming. How could the one person I love more than anything be so interconnected with the person most dangerous for me?

"Jake. You are amazing. This was amazing and I don't ever want to leave. But I still need to talk to you." He smiled a nervous smile as he hopped into his dark blue jeans, the ones which sculpted his body just so, undoubtedly the reason most girls in our school now hated me.

"Shoot." He was reclaiming his shirt from the other side of the room and I was distracted by the shape of him but the heaviness of my brief moments alone in the garage come weird meeting room clouded round all of my positive thoughts and happiness, sending them tumbling into oblivion with frightening ease.

"I told you I've have had more visions. Well there's more. Lots more." I was standing now, giving way to the potential need to escape with speed either from Jake's rejection or the arrival of Mr. Mayer. I had Jake's attention now, he slid back onto the couch like a kid being reprimanded, eyes suddenly filled with worry and disappointment, but he didn't speak.

"I wasn't visiting long lost family in Boston, and whatever you start to think now, it's nothing like that. But I am so sorry I lied, I didn't want to drag you into this, my mess. Everything is getting out of control and I wouldn't bring you in but I need you and suddenly it's got so close to home. I'm terrified and I need you, I just hope telling you this stuff won't mean I have to lose you." My babbling stream of consciousness fell from my mouth with absolutely no grace and his face fell as he tried to process it.

"Wow. That was a lot to take in Scarlett and quite a way to dampen the mood." The pause was long and I was afraid of what would come next. "Ok. So what were you doing in Boston that was so important you couldn't tell me?" He didn't seem angry, just sad, which was so much worse. My betrayal was burning him, I could see it.

I took the seat next to him and thrust my hands over his. He squeezed them back and I felt a small wave of relief wash over me. He hadn't instantly retracted his love so that was a start.

"My research, into my visions led to there. I went to visit someone who knew about gifts like mine. She had a letter for me. For me, written years ago by her friend who had the same gift. She knew my future and left a letter for me to find." Even to me it sounded insane.

He soaked up my words before looking up at me, confused. "What? Wait? She knew your future? Have you read it? You shouldn't mess with this stuff Scarlett. You need to live your life not have someone you don't know tell you what is going to happen." Frustration crept into his voice.

"I know it sounds crazy Jake, I feel crazy believe me." I noticed our hands were apart, he must have done that, a pain jabbed sharp in my chest. It was happening already.

"It's all true Jake. I am in danger. Girls like me have been disappearing for centuries, only now it's way more clever and secretive than before. There's a secret society called The Venari, they are all over Jake and they are closing in on me." His face erupted into a wry smile and it crushed me.

"This is crazy Scarlett. You sound crazy. They're after you? No-one knows but me and I haven't told anyone." By this point I was fighting back large tears as they pooled in my lids and weighted them til they gave way. I threw my hands to my face to hide my embarrassment. This time no comforting hand. The gap widened.

"I know. I know exactly what it sounds like, I'm not stupid Jake. You're not listening, there's more. Your dad…" A sob wracked my body and he seemed not to notice, hanging on the mention of his father in the midst of this madness.

"He's involved. The Venari, they're all people in power, people with influence and or money. They use it to make these girls; girls like me disappear by any means necessary." I was too scared to look up. He exhaled loudly; it was born from anger or exhaustion.

"How the hell did we get on to this? Are you hearing yourself?" His back turned he dragged tense outstretched fingers through his hair before punching the wall with a huge thud. Even sensing his obvious frustration I wasn't expecting what came next.

"You know what? I think you need to go. Now. I can't have this conversation with you, it's nuts. I am here for you with the visions and helping you stick it out at school, but you cannot come into my house and spout this crazy stuff about my dad and secret societies. That I can't deal with." He walked with purpose to the front door and held it open; his eyes fixed on something beyond me and waited.

My life had turned into a nightmare. This night, which until this point, and in spite of everything else could have been the best of my life, was spiraling into chaos. Despite being in the same room as him I had never felt more isolated and terrified. The one person I wanted close to me was the person pushing me away and I wasn't sure if I was mentally or emotionally strong enough to cope with this. I was basically raising myself these days too, so there was no-one else.

I wanted to speak as I brushed past but all I could utter was a low sob which forced more tears to cascade down my cheeks. I locked my eyes on his and for the first time since I had known him, there was nothing looking back, behind his eyes where there was normally such warmth and affection was now a void. He dipped his head and turned it away from mine sending another sharp stab of pure agony through my chest. I was broken.

"Look. I just don't wanna have this conversation, I think we need to cool off and I don't know, talk when you're in a better place." His gaze didn't return to mine, he pushed the door with a deafening click which sounded like the end of my world.

A crumbling person, I waded through such heavy sadness that I couldn't even imagine making it home, eyes blurry and throat narrow and dry. Waves of nausea washed over me repeatedly and I chastised myself over and over again for my poor judgment. What had I expected him to say? Then I remembered, the only thing I had needed the whole time was to show him the piece of paper that nestled in my jeans pocket. Though even then I would have had the unenviable task of admitting my breaking and entering as well as ongoing mentally unstable behavior.

Stairs like mountains, legs weak and frail I barely made it to my bed before breaking into thousands of tearful pieces. Whatever anyone said about your heartbreaking, it was worse. There were no words only a tangle of pain and my body's physical reaction to the emotional trauma. I had never heard of anyone actually being proven to die from a broken heart but they say it can happen and if that was true I was unquestionably next. My phone lay in my sweating palm, tauntingly silent and devoid of any consolation. I couldn't call him, even though I wanted only his voice, his arms, I couldn't fix this. I didn't know where to start.

Envelope two. Why wait? Even if Alice said they found me today, this night I couldn't care, they were welcome to me. Without his comfort I was a lost soul and the longing, such intense and dark longing was unbearable. I peeled back the paper, tears streaming from my face and fighting for breath. I had none of the same caution as last time, I was instead braced for whatever was coming, and it couldn't, in a million years, hurt more than this, than his rejection.

Scarlett... I know this much, there is little time. Something is changing and the confusion and doubt surrounding you will be lifted, it will be known and you will be targeted. I can't see what form it will take, how they will approach you, but I know you are special. The one with all the knowledge and power to bring them down. Your gifts too are not to be dismissed, you must focus your emotions, channel them into understanding yourself, you can control them, use them as tools to help you. This is something only you can do, I never learnt how to properly harness my own, but I knew girls who could and I know, without a trace of doubt you are by far the most powerful of us all. Find your muse. Find your strength and focus.

Alice x

No comfort to be found there either. I still knew nothing about my visions; I couldn't control them, stop them or escape from them and now I was at the mercy of a bunch of narrow-minded fools whose goal was to bring me down for something I didn't even want. I felt broken.

I screwed up the paper and threw it as hard as I could across the room. Trapped inside my life I buried my head into the quilt and despite the obvious impending danger I thought only of him. What was he thinking right now? How did he think this would get better? How could it have all changed so fast? I knew this; I had proof of what they were doing, so as long as I could keep that safe until I knew more I could eventually make sure everyone knew what these so called pillars of society were doing.

The Internet seemed the most logical place for answers of any type and there was nothing to stop me crying while I searched. Clayton Mayer. He had his own bio page on the Salem town directory site, a real family man. The picture of his face staring back at me froze my core, but in a small way it helped, it moved a tiny part of my sadness and turned it to a burning rage like I had never known. If I could harness that I would have a better chance.

Clayton Mayer with three golf buddies. Pictured were Stan Carmichael, a balding, round-faced Attorney, Mason Clees, a tall, dark and angular Chief of Police and Edward Sutcliffe, former Chief of Staff at Danvers Mental Health Facility. His name whirred in my head, he was older than the others, by about fifteen years but that name; it was him. These were the ones I knew I had to be most wary of; these were the Venari, the ones with all the power they needed between them to steal me away, torture me and make it look like some kind of deadly accident. Still crying, though more silently and defeated. My breath was fighting to escape and my heart pounded furiously. I pressed print and watched my hand shake as I extended it to grab the picture; one filled with evil, mocking eyes.

Sat in my bed, surrounded with my notes and books I tried coherent thought. My pen raced across the page and back again, from the beginning, what I had seen, where, Jake's kind reaction, his father's strange one. The books, the notes from the exhibition, the green notebook, the trip to Boston. All of my passing comments, details from the lodge, the comfort from my host whose name I still left out in case, I didn't want her blood on my hands, it all flooded from a me with surprising ease. It was therapy, but it was security. My mind slightly sharper and driven to anger I scrawled everything I could think of, leading my unknown reader to the clues I had found myself, spelling it all out in graphic detail. The witch hunt never ended but one way or another I was stopping this madness.

I must have cried and written myself into exhaustion. I woke with the curtains open but the sky dark; trees outside waved witch-like hands of shadow across the yard and into my room where they stretched and danced across the ceiling in the winds which had picked up since winter began to approach. I peered outside to the front of the house; Mom's car was still gone, another all-nighter, not even a courtesy call this time, perhaps she wouldn't notice if I just ran away. For a brief moment it seemed plausible, Betty, well Annie had done it, evaded them for so long, what's to say I couldn't?

I dismissed the thought almost instantly. The idea of being away from here, from Jake, tightened the knot in my gut. I would rather face whatever they had for me than lose proximity, which was about all I had right now. My phone taunted me in the dim light, nothing.

I flicked on the lamp and completed my story so far; hastily written scribbling's of a lunatic I should have called it. But right now, this was very real and my demons grew stronger, drawing nearer.

The street beyond our drive was silent and the lights played to an empty street as everyone slept. The quiet was disrupted by the engine of a single car which grew closer; but instead of fading peacefully into the night it seemed to linger. I turned off the lamp and crept to the window. With my curtain as a shield I peered round to see the car, engine running, poised at the start of our driveway. The driver, head turned but shrouded in darkness, was looking directly at me. I flashed a glance at my alarm clock, three am. Who the hell would be here at this time? For one moment I allowed myself to think it, Jake had come to talk to me, knowing I would be tossing and turning after our fight. I squinted to make out the face in the poor light and a bolt of white hot panic flowed through my entire body. His eyes boring a hole into my hidden face; he was watching, waiting. Clayton Mayer didn't flinch, or move at all. In an act deliberately designed to evoke this exact reaction he remained perfectly still, unnervingly so.

I couldn't look away, though I wanted to. Not looking would have made me feel even more vulnerable. The door. I didn't lock it when I came home, I was so desperate to leave the night behind I couldn't be sure I have even closed it. I ran, as fast as my feet could carry me through the dark house; it felt more like a prison and less like home than ever as my feet landed on its alien floorboards. I flicked the switch on the lock and collapsed in a heap behind the door, head below the glass panels that had alarming potential to reveal my hiding place. I could hear the engine turning over and over again, the white noise becoming engrained on my mind. Then with a slow burst of the accelerator he was gone. I daren't move and stayed hunched on the spot for what felt like hours, frozen in fear.

My heart stopped as the gravel on the drive crunched below wheels, he was back. I tried to make it to the kitchen, but my body was paralysed. I curled myself so tight I could feel my heartbeat against my hunched knees. My breathing careered from huge rushed gasps to shallow, strained breaths that seemed barely enough to sustain a person.

I knew a shadow loomed in the doorway, I felt the light around me change with its approach and thought I was going to be sick. The door rattled and I still couldn't move. Then I heard a familiar sound, keys. Mom. I shuffled away from the door's range and clung to the stairs. The sense of relief was immense but it had sent my heightened emotions over the edge and before she even managed to walk in I was sobbing uncontrollably.

She gasped with fright. "Scarlett honey. What on earth are you doing? You scared the life out of me. What's wrong sweetie, tell me what it is?" She sat down next to me and cradled my head like she used to when I fell off my bike or grazed my knee and wished so hard for it to be something that simple.

Words left me again. I was a hysterical mute, my cries so extreme they became silent fights for air. I was shaking, she was frightened.

"You need to tell me what has happened sweetie. Breathe." She tightened her grip in an attempt to make me feel safe but it wasn't enough, I wasn't safe, not even with her.

I still hadn't said anything, and part of me thought maybe I shouldn't. It seemed only to make things worse and I knew she had her suspicions about my behavior since we moved. My vocal chords strained and I only managed to utter incomprehensible sounds between huge sobs.

"Right. I am calling the doctor." She scrambled for her phone and starting punching numbers in from her diary. She left me on the stairs and paced the front room as she made the call. Her voice was muffled and I was still fighting to breathe. I caught her apology for the hour and sensed the urgency in her voice. She rushed back to where I was sprawled in the hall and sat back down.

"Mr. Mayer is coming over. He is going to make it all better. Whatever it is darling, I swear it will be ok." From the silence, huge terrified screams burst from my throat and I hauled myself to my feet, running to my room. I scraped my notes up from the bed, tore the paper from my pocket and hurriedly crouched to find them a hiding place away from them, him.

The darkness under my bed was cooler than the air above. I felt the floor shift slightly beneath my hands. A loose floorboard I hadn't seen it before, it was fate. I shook it free from its neighboring slats and I slid the pages into the space below my hands where the air was cold and damp. Grit and dirt gathered under my fingernails as I pushed until I couldn't reach any further. He wasn't far now; the threat of his approaching hatred and ignorance clung to the heavy air and added to my growing sense of claustrophobia. This wasn't just about me, what I could do, it went much deeper. Governed by fear, he groped for answers he wasn't willing to accept and his conclusion was clear - my kind was not to be tolerated.

Somewhere on my bizarre hunt for answers I had lined myself up for capture and my missteps were about to cost me everything. Aware that the events consuming me were about to come to a sinister climax, I did the only thing I could think of. I wrapped myself in my own arms, pulled my knees up to my chin and waited in the dark.

Mom didn't join me in my room; I sat without the lights and listened to her incoherent crying and talking in the hall. She shouted up at me; "Scarlett, you are really scaring me now. What the hell is going on?" She was shaking and he voice broke as she spoke.

"Mom. I don't want to see him. I don't need to see him. I need you to listen to me." My voice powered with purpose seemed to return from nowhere. I wiped the damp tear tracks away from my face with the back of my hand. "Call him. Tell him not to come. NOW!" She appeared in the doorframe.

"Well I think you're wrong Scarlett. I think you do need to see him. Something is going on. You're sobbing in an empty house, shouting and screaming at me for no reason. This is not normal behavior and quite frankly I don't know what to do with you anymore. You're like a stranger."

She slumped onto my bed like she had lost a fight, exhausted and beaten, her head fell into her hands and she wiped sad tears away from her eyes.

Then the crackle of stone chips under rubber filled my room and I knew it was too late. Mom jumped up and rushed to let him in. Like a rat trapped I jumped up from my foetal position desperately trying to think of ways to get out. My windows were too high, the fall would almost certainly break my legs, and they had the stairs covered. Their footsteps were already climbing, counting down will a dull percussion to my capture.

His figure appeared in my room. Why hadn't I at least locked the damn door? Mom wasn't with him, part of the plan I am sure. He would have convinced her in a hushed tone that this was better for me, without her there. He hit the lights causing me to wince in the brightness at it stung my exhausted eyes.

"Scarlett." It wasn't a greeting it was an acknowledgment. I knew he knew what I had found out. Perhaps I left the garage door ajar or didn't lock the cabinet properly; whatever it was that gave me away, he knew. It was like everything else; he had so much on me and I had no idea how? I recalled those first few encounters, the looks and the feeling of unease. Even then he knew more about me than I could understand.

His sinister gaze took in my room; maybe he was searching for signs of the occult, or looking for something to restrain me with. I said nothing. He walked with heavy steps over to me and reached out a hand, I backed into the window but his hand was wound tightly around my wrist. I let out a scream and tried with all the energy I could summon to wrestle free but his touch burned my twisting skin and pain spread across my arm.

In his other hand was a leather bag, an old style doctor's case which had a kind of domed top. He placed it with a creepy calm onto my bed and yanked my weak frame towards him. His strength was terrifying. I couldn't move and I didn't know what was coming. Mom was nowhere to be heard or seen, she had handed me to them on a plate without even realizing. That was their trick, their own black magic. By convincing her I was mad, it didn't even matter if I told the truth, she would never believe me anyway.

He spoke. His voice quiet but dark and firm. "I think we both know why I am here Scarlett. And I hoped I was wrong about you, at least for Jake's sake, but you know we can't allow someone like you, especially someone who knows so much, someone who can do so much to just wander the streets." Do so much? I hadn't been able to do anything.

"I don't know what you're talking about." I lied, badly, my trembling voice revealing the truth.

Shaking his head slowly, he smirked. "Oh I think you do." I screamed for my mom, several times but she never came. He must have said to stay away no matter what she heard; I refused to believe she would willingly neglect me so cruelly. He was doing just what they had said the Venari did; manipulate weak, emotionally wrought parents into handing over complete control of their 'vulnerable' children.

His right hand, which had been fumbling around in his cavernous bag appeared into my view holding a syringe. My eyes widened and let out another futile scream. The pain in my arm grew stronger as I tried desperately to shift my body away from his. He moved quickly, expelling the air from the needle's end as he leaned towards me.

Without a word, but with a loaded, dark stare, he plunged the needle into my arm. The hot pin prick was followed by a cold, rush of solution which coursed with speed into my adrenaline fuelled veins.

"What are you going to do…?" I felt my voice trail off, it was almost instant. My vision became blurred and sparkly like my life had suddenly become animated. He was speaking but my ears wouldn't let the sound in. His voice was stilted and low like a CD slowed right down or a robot running out of power.

The light dimmed and I was lying down. I could feel my body but I had no control over it. I couldn't move it. I was literally trapped inside myself. Whatever was in the syringe had paralysed me. I felt him lift me, my eyes stared forward but I couldn't even blink and the shapes and sights were merged into blocks of shape and color. I could hear muffled sobs from my mom and his voice spoke back.

Suddenly, we were in his car. All three of us, well at this time I barely classed as a person. My hearing fluctuated; I caught words here and there. Drive. Hospital, my first thought was at least Danvers was closed. Treatment. End to it. End to what? My life? My heart still pounded and I was aware of movement around me, it was like an out of body experience. I could almost see the scene from above. It crossed my mind that I might already be dead and stuck in some kind of hideous limbo but the occasional word broke through and assured me I was alive, alive but totally powerless and I couldn't decide which was worse.

I had heard about this kind of thing, people trapped in their own minds. Perfectly capable of coherent thought but outwardly appearing as if in a comatose state and I felt a stab of total fear. What if I never woke up? What if this was my life now? My mind wandered from the trivial: this isn't the last outfit I would have chosen if I had known today was the end, to the more serious: I would never get married, never kiss Jake again or prove to him that I am not mad. This was the worst of all. Thinking I may never touch his face or smell his scent was the hardest blow and my heart ached inside my frozen chest.

BATTLE

The lights were brighter there and my open eyes ached but refused to shut. My hearing had improved and I was grabbing more sentences than just words now. My mom sat by me, I felt her hand on mine and she uttered "I love you," over and over again between apologies and trembling sobs.

The smell of disinfectant filled my nose and the clinical air of a hospital was unmistakable. It seemed odd to bring me here, so public; surely not everyone would be on his side or approve of his unorthodox injections into teenage patients.

I felt him enter the room, that cold feeling he gave me was even able to penetrate my suspended state. He wasn't in the periphery of my poor vision but I could hear him almost perfectly now.

"I have called in a favor," he spoke low and soft. I assumed addressing my mom. "They are going to let a friend of mine come in and act as her doctor. He is semi-retired but a specialist in this kind of episode, I mentioned him a while back when we first discussed her, issues." Issues. He was a monster.

My mom didn't say anything; I could only guess she must have nodded. He obviously received some kind of acknowledgment as he kept talking. His voice turned my stomach and I willed my disobedient body to life. To no avail. My hearing was the only thing that had improved at all. I couldn't feel my legs and had only the vaguest of sensation in my hands, but no movement.

"His name is Dr. Sutcliffe. He will be here within the hour. They will keep her sedated for now and hopefully we can get to the bottom of this for you." Sutcliffe. I was going to go the same way as Alice, he was going to eradicate me like a pest, no doubt lock me up in some other hellhole institution.

I had moved beyond fear to anger. It coursed through my motionless body and in my head I was screaming, screaming for Jake to work it out. I remember what Alice had said that I needed to find my muse and focus. He was it; he was everything and right now my only hope.

I filled my mind with all the images of him. The day he walked into the cafeteria. How he mentioned my hair in class, saved me at the dance. The time we kissed in the car and just yesterday when we had been together, how he wanted me and loved me. I poured every ounce of that feeling he gave me into focusing my energy. I could smell the skin on his neck and feel his hands on mine. I closed in on the image of his face and pressed my mind to come up with something. I would not die here.

There it was, the drunk, tingly feeling I got when my visions were coming. Only all I could see was his room. I had only been in it once, briefly, but I knew it and I could smell his clothes, his skin. I could see through his eyes, then the hospital lights bleached out my mind's eye and I lost it.

I couldn't be sure if it was desperation and that I had wanted it so badly or if I had been able to work my mind, take control of it like Alice said. I remembered the first journal, the girl whose boyfriend had seen what she saw and I was determined to show him the way. I had never focused my mind like this and I didn't know what it would take to show him something but I had to believe in my ability and our connection. I just needed enough to stir his curiosity before Sutcliffe could take me away from here, for all I knew there could be a range to my ability and a mile or so away might be too far for me to try communicate with him. It had to be now.

I tried again. Summoning all the mental images I had of him with such rabid determination my head ached and I felt my muscles tense further. I lost my vision to that within my head and I sat it within reach, his room, the scent of him returned and I grasped with everything shred of myself to keep the picture alive.

It became clearer, I was doing it. I was seeing through his eyes, his hands grasped his phone and I made out my name on the screen. He was thinking about me. I spoke silently to him, willing him to hear my voice. He didn't move and I couldn't feel any reaction. I tried again.

Jake. Please hear me. Please. I wasn't lying, I need you, quickly. I felt his body shift and his eyes darted upwards. It felt like he was listening to me. My heart's ever escalating pace picked up further. You need to go to my house, I'm in trouble. Read the papers Jake. Read all of them, you have to, to understand. And then all of a sudden I lost him. The hospital returned and I couldn't be sure if he had got my message or not. I was crying. Defunct tear ducts kept my misery locked inside and I lay there, powerless.

I lost all sense of time. It could have been hours or days; the fluorescent lights seemed never to dim and people came and went. Mom had barely left my side but someone convinced her to leave and rest, she fought but Mr.. Mayer butted in and took control of the situation as usual.

Not long after she had kissed my head and left I heard his breath in my ear. "Scarlett. I know you can hear me. Do not try anything with that sick little mind of yours. Our good friend Mr.. Sutcliffe will be here soon and we can make this all. Go. Away." He sounded so damaged, his sinister voice echoed in my troubled head. With that he left and I was alone.

I must have been drifting in an out of sleep, punctuated with panicked waking and renewed terror about being locked inside myself. No Jake, no Mom and no comfort. Tears wanted to fall again but my body refused to let them.

Exhaustion and my inability to move meant I had drifted in and out of weak sleep. When my eyes opened next I was somewhere else. The lights were clearer now; the cocktail must have been wearing off. The movement was back in my neck, though I was struggling to shift my hands and feet. I looked down, grateful for the chance to move at all and saw my limbs shackled with thick, worn leather straps which pinned me to the bed. This was a modern day witch hunt and I was tied to a stake.

I was propped up on pillows and still felt drowsy and limp. I looked around, the white starchiness of the hospital replaced with a green hue and equally chemical smell. The room was all breeze blocks, poorly painted with olive paint, it was oppressive and claustrophobic. The door had a small closed hatch and a single mirror was inset into the wall to my left.

An asylum. I knew it, if not by instinct from the words Alice had used to describe her own prison. I could hear faint cries and screams and it was worse than a horror movie. Footsteps occasionally passed by my door but never stopped, coupled with the haunting squeak of ancient gurney wheels. Then the hatch dropped down with a clank, shaking me from the nightmares I was playing out in my mind. A new pair of eyes shot me a withering look and it snapped shut as key fumbled in the iron lock.

In came the man I felt I knew but wished I didn't. Alice's descriptions, the picture I had discovered online. He was worse than Mr. Mayer, which seemed impossible. His entrance brought the room down by a couple of degrees whether that was psychological or just a rush of air from the corridor beyond I couldn't be sure but the chill chased the line of my spine and I shivered.

He held my gaze and his aggressive, pointed face broke into a crooked smile to reveal gross, yellowing teeth. He pulled up a plastic chair from the other side of the room with a lingering, high-pitched sound that pierced my brain. He positioned himself uncomfortably close to me.

"I have been waiting to meet you Scarlett. Alice spoke fondly of you. Seems she had a lot of information about you. Yes, she mentioned you once or twice when she was sedated. It has been a long wait." He relaxed back into the chair like this was the most normal situation in the world.

I didn't speak; instead I turned my head away to face the breezeblocks. His hand grabbed my face and pulled it with force to face him.

"That's very rude Scarlett. You shouldn't look away when people are talking to you." His voice rasped as his hands tightly grasped at my cheeks, his bony fingers bruising my skin.

"I suppose you won't talk. They often don't. Do understand there are things that can be done about that now you are in my charge. It would serve you well to remember that." He released his grip and stood. Pacing around the room he proceeded to talk in riddles about what he was going to do to me. How he was going to remove the threat I posed.

"Your mother already suspected you had deep, complex mental issues, so you have done half the job for us. Right at this moment she thinks I am performing a comprehensive mental assessment on you. And guess what..?" His eyes lit up and his eyebrows moved up with delight.

"I will tell her you need constant care and sedation. Then of course you will deteriorate. We will try doing everything we can, but, what tragedy. You will plummet to such a low that the only option was to take your own life. That's what they'll know out there. You'll have simply, disappeared. At that point we can decide what best to do with you."

He was playing out my fate like some kind of sick puppet master and I was locked up here. I wrenched my body from side to side in a futile attempt to escape; he laughed and brought his eyes back to mine. "The Venari takes its work very seriously Scarlett. We have survived for centuries without being revealed and we will not allow someone like you to reveal our secret. No matter how impressive your skills may turn out to be. We have and will continue to go to any lengths to stop that happening." My skills?

I wanted to scream at him, tell him about the trail I had left, the information, but I knew that would mean they could get to it, destroy it and I still hoped Jake may have heard enough to get to it.

"I don't die here." I bluffed, some feigned confidence welled up from my chest and I spoke with conviction. He laughed again but didn't speak, hands rubbing at his chin while he paced and thought.

"I have seen it. I live a long and happy life and your kind, you animals, you are unveiled for what you really are and the Venari die. It's over." I spoke with such venom I almost convinced myself. The words hissed through my clenched teeth.

He cocked his head up quickly and strode over to me. The back of his right hand collided violently with my face, the contact left my cheek hot and the reminder of his touch remained.

"Stop this nonsense. You haven't seen anything of worth yet. You are a frightened little girl and you have no idea what you are dealing with." With that he stormed out of the room and slammed the door. I had managed to penetrate his confidence even if only slightly. I found myself alone, but somehow no longer scared. Maybe I was stronger than I thought, or maybe I had given up and accepted what was coming to me. Either way I didn't want to cry anymore, I couldn't find another tear if I tried.

Whitehaven Lodge MA. That's what is said printed on the hideous robes I was wearing. I couldn't have been so far from home then, but it felt like a million miles.

I retreated to my mind and I forced myself to focus. Jake, where are you? I couldn't summon his view like before, it just wouldn't come. I concentrated as hard as I could; the pain flooded my head as I exerted myself to make some progress.

For the first time I relished what I knew was coming. My limbs weakened and I knew I was going to have one. I used those precious moments before to pray, I never prayed but this seemed like the time to try. Please let it be one. I need to see something to know I make it through this.

When my body was limp and my vision cleared I was in my room at home. There was no one there but the floorboard I had used to hide my discoveries lay on my bed and the papers I knew held the key to ending this nightmare were strewn all over my bed. I wasn't sure whether to be terrified or relieved. The outcome depended entirely on who had found them.

I woke wearily from my other life and found myself still stuck in the olive hell, horrifying sounds still made their way under the door and into my ears. I hummed to myself, a lullaby my mom sang to me as a kid and turned the volume up in my head to drown them out.

The next thing I felt was a sharp pain, my arm. Two people in surgical masks towered over me and medical machinery beeped and pulsed in the background. I knew the two pairs of eyes that looked into mine and my stomach knotted further. I struggled again but the straps from before were fastened tighter around my limbs and had been accompanied by a large band across my abdomen to make absolutely sure I couldn't get out.

A hand lurched over me with a mask, headed towards my face and Dr. Meyer, eyes spread into a smile, spoke: "Soon it will all be over Scarlett." What would be over? Me? The experimentation? I screamed but the sound had gone again and the mask was covering my nose and mouth. I tried not to breathe. I held my breath until my chest felt like it might explode and I found myself involuntarily gasping, sucking in their toxicity. My eyes lulled and I fell into darkness, I was sure of it. This was death felt like.

THE OTHER SIDE

My hands collected every shred they could find. I stuffed them frantically in to the bag and crept downstairs so not to be discovered. In the car the bag called to me and I wanted to open it now and put the pieces together but I needed to be somewhere safe. My vision was blurry and I didn't know what I was doing, this didn't feel like me. If this was limbo or hell it seemed disconcertingly like everyday life, a strange thought and I didn't know whether to be relieved or saddened. My eyes flashed up at the rear view mirror and I felt my absent body jolt. Jake's brown eyes stared back. I was seeing what Jake was seeing. He had found the information, but there was little time. I needed him to understand it, absorb it and get help before it was too late.

We were driving and I sensed he knew I was there with him. I had done it, somehow in my drug induced state I had found him, the connection between us strong enough to endure through everything, I loved him more than ever right now and prayed he found the whole me before it was too late. He pulled over as soon as he was off my street.

"Jake, you are freaking crazy? Hearing voices, breaking into your girlfriend's house." He shuffled the pages and I felt his mind work through my notes. His breathing quickened as he took in the information Alice had left me and I felt the echo of his guilt as he realized I had been telling the truth. The pain of our last encounter was resurrected within me and I felt the need to cry but my body wouldn't allow it.

The next page was the paper I took from his dad. Part of me was sad, I didn't want to ruin his father for him, but on the other hand, he had a right to know what a monster he lived with. His breath was held as he took in each word. He stopped at his father's name and brought a shaking hand to his mouth. He punched the windshield so hard a small crack forked in several directions before throwing the paper down onto the seat and bringing his cell into view. He stabbed angrily at the key pad and his chest heaved with rage.

"Pick up you bastard." His feet tapped impatiently on the mat below. The phone at his ear rang and rang. I felt the impulse to hang up surge through him but he held on and that second a voice answered and I heard it as Jake and from the room I was in as if I had literally split myself in two.

"Jake, I am just in the middle of something. Can I..." Mr.. Mayer could sense the anger and was hoping to diffuse the situation before it arose. Too late.

"Where is she?" Jake bellowed with such fury I felt the vibrations in my own head. Unphased his dad replied as if he had asked him what was for dinner.

"What are you talking about Jake? I really don't have time for this." Mayer let out a sigh and Jake cut him short again.

"Scarlett. What have you done with Scarlett Dad? I know all about your sick little club, to think I stood up for you. You're a sick freak and I am going to kill you if you touch her. I swear to God..." With that he was about to hang up when something bleeped. My heart was failing and the machine sounded the alarm, the picture crackled like a TV with no reception and I could barely see. Jake caught the sound but I couldn't sense what happened next, whether or not he worked it out, if he'd find me. The dark crept back in.

Somehow I was still hanging on; though I knew I was weak and the various layers of drugs they had been feeding me were crippling my organs. I felt sick, deep, sharp pains ran the length of my body; I didn't know how much longer I could hang on for. Convulsive shakes gripped me.

My eyes were closed but my hearing was back. I was still in the same room but the machine had stopped its high pitched beeping, at least my heart was working.

"Jake knows." His voice was heavy and more human than I had ever heard it before. If I wasn't lying half dead on an operating table at his hands I may have felt sorry for him.

"Well Clay, if he really does you know the protocol. We finish up here then we need to track him down as soon as possible. We need to end this." He meant us, me and Jake. We were too powerful with the knowledge we now shared and he was planning to wipe us both out. The idea of me dying was uncomfortable but the idea of anyone stealing that life, his life, was unbearable. I searched my mind for the signal, trying to connect to him but my chance had gone. I was too weak and I had no way of warning him.

I lay there, taking in each word. Instruments chinked on metal trays and their feet padded around the linoleum flooring. What were they doing? From the silence a commotion so dramatic occurred so fast if I had been alert and watching I sense I may have suffered some kind of stress-related trauma.

I heard the doors slam with force into the wall. Raised voices flooded my ears but one sound stood out clear, Jake.

"Jesus Christ Dad, what they hell are you into. What is this?" Footsteps of the two men surrounding me waded cautiously away in Jake's direction.

"Jake. How did you? Calm down, son." Clayton's voice was as measured and dead as ever. The darkness in him escaping in his tone; he really thought this was ok.

"Do. Not. Call me that. Is she...what have you done to her? GPS you idiot... your phone." His voice was quaking. I wanted so much to reach out and hold him. I cursed my body for its betrayal and lay there, a silent witness to my own end.

Sutcliffe joined in the fun. "Jake. You need to put the gun down." Gun? Please let me move, please let me just wake up and help him. Nothing.

"Don't tell me what I need to do. You two sick creeps need to burn for what you've done." There was a sudden shuffle of feet and they were grappling, grunting and wrestling around. Metal trays clattered to the floor with a crash, a temporary pause before they pressed on. I felt one of them edge closer, cautiously, surreptitiously and the familiar white hot pain of a needle in my arm, more drugs. I wouldn't survive more.

I could make out Jake's troubled breaths as he fought them off, he landed a punch and Sutcliffe fell to the floor with a groan. Feet jostled against each other and words were being hissed, deep and low. I couldn't make them out. Then a sound which forced a jet of hot bile up from my stomach into my throat. A single shot. Silence. There was no sound, nothing. I wanted to die then, if he was gone I didn't want to fight back from this abyss I was in, I should just let go. The warm advance of my latest injection was started to topple my senses again and I felt like I was spinning.

My suffering interrupted by the sound of a gasp and one set of feet running back through the doors where Jake had made his entrance, they disappeared down the corridor and my ears traced them as far as they would go.

Two left. Silence filled the room and I willed my eyes open but my body continued to reject my pleas. There was a faint sound, someone stood up, two fingers against my throat to check my pulse, pushed hard into my neck. The straps on my ankles were being yanked, aggressively, then my abdomen, then my wrists. Then there was more unknown. I was an intermittent human; barely there, fighting the dark that I could only assume was death beckoning, urging me just to let go. I was too lost in an abyss of pitch black. Occasionally pin holes of sound or sensation from outside of my mind broke through and although I couldn't properly see or hear the real world, I felt like I may well not want to. My poor, strained heart pounded like a drum.

The world became nauseatingly unsettled as I swirled and drifted between shadows and shapes and light mixing beyond my locked eyelids flashed and pulsed. It didn't feel like real seeing, just more of being lost in some odd no-mans-land. I was in some semi-nightmare and felt like I was the only passenger on a turbulent flight. I didn't know what was real but I was sure the smell of chemicals faded and a cool breeze hit my face. How? The might-be air or a cruel trick of my imagination whistled around me as I was thrown like a rag doll, more turbulence and all I could manage to think was that if my gnawing fear of who had made it out was to be confirmed; my ability to fend of the advances of the dark would be pointless and my shattered soul would disappear. Wherever I might be going I had left my life in pieces behind me.

I was awash with locked-in grief and sick from the constant movement. The ride to the afterlife was certainly unpleasant and so, so long.

I started to feel tingles as the feeling returned to my fingers and toes but I dared not move them, dead was probably better. It was spreading and I knew I could probably open my eyes but I was too scared. My hearing crept back in with painful bursts of muffled sound. A car. That explained the turbulence. It stopped. There were several minutes of almost silence; just patchy sounds hard to make out. I heard the flick of the keys in the ignition and as if my ears had popped on a descent all the sounds were amplified. It was just us, two people in a small, claustrophobic space.

The nothing was broken by a deep, heart wrenching sob and my mind whirled over the noise, processing as fast as it could after such a trauma what this meant. Jake. That sound was Jake. I opened my eyes, and though they were heavy and sore I could see the back of his neck hunched over the steering wheel. My body was impossibly weak and I could hardly blink let alone reach for him.

He was breaking down, I watched for a moment, so grateful to be alive, to be with him that I remained paralysed. I couldn't move, but I managed an almost inaudible sentence: "I'm so sorry." It came out as a whisper but it broke his cry and he spun round.

"Oh my god, Scarlett. You're alive. I really thought..." He leapt over the seat and pulled my head up into his knee. "I'm so sorry I didn't believe you. I could have stopped all of this and I didn't listen. I'm so sorry. He kissed my forehead over and over and then we both said nothing, we just clung to each other and cried, hard, grateful tears.

FUTURE

Blue lights had encircled our house for the entire evening so I was sure the neighbors were getting their own back for my constant peering into their business.

My notes, the information I gathered, were gathered up by officious looking police officers who shot me more than a few furtive, almost apologetic glances. Recent experiences made it hard for me to trust those in power, for fairly obvious reasons and I tried to reign in my thoughts about them plotting to finish what the others started.

I shot a furtive glance at Jake as we hovered in my doorway. He flashed me a conspiratorial nod and I knew in that second that he had kept it safe; the information which could bring the whole terrible truth out. The officers were satisfied they had it all, but they only had the weakest clues and there was no way they could piece together the lineage of The Venari from that. Really, who would believe it?

Hundreds of years pass and our apparent tolerance is a thin veil for one of the most exquisitely evil abuses of power ever uncovered. No, no-one in their right mind would swallow that. Bar me; though perhaps I was being a little optimistic putting myself in the sound-mind camp.

Downstairs my mom stirred coffees for the officers while they traded their shock and disgust about Chief of Police Mason Clees and his links with the Venari 'cult' as they called it. Sutcliffe, the owner of the footsteps I had heard running away from the room, was still missing and Jake's dad had been found dead from his injuries. Strangely I felt numb. I didn't want Jake to have lost his father, but I was unable to conjure the sadness usually associated with an unexpected death. For me it was more like a weight had been lifted. I was free, at least for now. I felt bad when I thought about him though; Jake had some tough times coming. It hadn't hit him yet, what had really happened and I was bracing myself for whatever may be around the corner. I didn't know if it would be grief, or perhaps anger? How do you begin to process finding out that your father was a monster? He was an orphan at eighteen; the sadness of that thought was almost too much to bear and I wanted to just hold him, constantly as I reminded myself of how amazingly lucky I was to have my own parents, and for the chance to see them again.

I sat on the stoop, breathing in the cold evening air and felt Jake's arms curl round my back. He had been apologising and kissing me every second since we got home. My mom had been the same and it was clear she didn't really know the extent of it, or that she couldn't accept it. We didn't discuss why he had taken me there or what it meant. Instead we both chose to relish the fact I was back; that was easier and I wanted that for her, the simplest understanding. This wasn't her burden to carry.

I felt strangely calm. I knew the danger wasn't gone, Sutcliffe was bad enough but at this point I had been through so much I felt like all I needed to be happy was to have Jake. I had been given my chance to breathe him in again, in those dark moments that was all I asked for and it was worth it, he was worth it. Anyway, Sutcliffe would have needed to be completely insane to show his face here again, even more insane than he obviously was.

When the light faded and the patrol cars pulled away, it was eerily silent. Mom was trying to be normal, washing up and offering to make my choice of dinner. Jake was clinging to me, which I loved, but none of us felt like talking about it. I think we all just took the time to contemplate how lucky we were.

"I think I'll just go sit on the bridge for a little while." Before Mom could utter the words I grabbed Jake's hand, I guessed I had to expect not to be allowed anywhere alone, possibly ever again.

We cuddled up in the fading light and took in the sound of the river passing, comforted by its continuity.

Jakes embrace was firm and safe. The iridescent glow of fairy lights, a welcome reminder that Christmas was coming, brought hope as they twinkled in the kitchen and made it almost impossible to comprehend how much had happened, how much had changed in just a few days.

Jake had been quiet since we made it back, his beautiful eyes weighted with guilt. Some of it was for me, some for his dad. He had taken a long time with the officers before, and was expected to go and make his full statement in the morning, but for now we were working through the unbelievable events together, leaning on each other whenever the scale of the shock or emotion threatened to knock us down.

He looked at me, eyes still so wrenched with pain. I put my hands on his face they way I always did and kissed him. That magic he had was still there, and I looked right back at him so glad it hadn't been extinguished by any of the complex emotions surrounding us. "Let's not talk about it tonight hey? One day, when the time is right for us both, but just not now." He just smiled back and squeezed me a little tighter; I took that to be a yes.

"Ok, but before we don't talk about it. I saved this. I didn't want them to take it in case you wanted it." He pulled the final small folded letter from his shirt pocket, wax intact. I stared at it, thinking of all that Alice knew and had told me, and where I had been for knowing it. The temptation to open it was still so huge and curiosity returned to burn in my finger tips. I shocked myself by even contemplating it after everything and a strong scent of the hospital chemicals rose to the fore of my mind. Surely a message from my mind, which still had so far to go before recovering wholly from the nightmare.

I ran back into the kitchen, grabbed the one thing I needed to do this right and rejoined Jake on the bridge.

I struck the match. I held it against the paper and watched as Alice's words flickered into amber, then to black. Jake put an arm around my waist and we watched together as the embers of the ashy page became weighted with water, were extinguished and floated away down the river.

I looked up at him with a smile. "Sometimes it's better just to live."

As I inhaled him, the mysterious, divine providence that had delivered us from such hideousness was the only thing I could think of. I was just… having those feelings, not the good kind. My joy and comfort instantly lost to the familiar bow of my knees, blurring of my vision. Why now? My pleas fell on deaf ears whoever had been there for me had gone and I was lost.

I had experienced this before; a vision but the body wasn't mine. I was wearing someone else and peering out through alien eyes on another scene. My body immersed in the premonition was still able to feel the emotions stirred by these eyes. I knew without reflection or the sound of his voice who this was and the scale of my revulsion shook me. Sick. I felt sick, the me that was trapped inside him retched. My skin grew clammy and I willed myself out. It didn't work and the weird voyeuristic play of my life unfolded in front of my borrowed eyes.

My hair was glowing in the dusk, an unintentional beacon ablaze in the dimming light and I felt a smirk to rise across his face as he watched us talking. I could hear his thoughts, with terrifying clarity. He was thinking about it, what was next. I didn't want to know. I wanted to be free. An unparalleled rage and frustration burned in his fingertips and he deftly worked the keypad on an old fashioned cell. As the tone played out he rubbed grazes that peppered his knuckles with his other hand; he wanted more than a little pay back.

He, we spoke hurried and low, he was trying to avoid being seen, or heard. "They've gone. She is alive, so is the boy. No, he didn't make it." He spoke cautiously and his eyes followed the distant me and he shifted as we watched my body turn toward our spying spot. "Get me the next steps. I don't care how long we wait but I want that information and I want it now. We cannot afford another incident like this. It could be catastrophic. Make sure the paperwork lines up; we must not be implicated. And bring forward the date for the new facility. We may need it sooner than we thought." Facility?

He was excited; I felt his pulse racing and his breath

quicken. His final thought as the vision flickered in a bid to fade was the worst. The excitement of the hunt to come coursed through the veins in his skin and he rubbed his hands together to rid them of a chill. His words resonated through the both of us as he spoke; "This is going to be very interesting indeed."

I returned to my life limp in Jake's arms; that all too recognizable terror on his face. "Scarlett? Scarlett? What? Tell me?" I fought against Jake's attentive hands as he tried to help me up, but I was too focused on the vision. I stared beyond the bridge and the curve of the river and searched.

"They're watching."

The Salem Witch Trials

In the spring of 1692 a group of young girls changed the course of the town's history forever.

It all started when the Reverend Parris' daughter Elizabeth, age 9, along with his niece Abigail Williams, age 11, started having what were described as 'fits'. They screamed and they threw things, they made peculiar sounds and twisted their bodies into all manner of strange positions. Crucially, the local doctor put the blame for what he witnessed firmly on the supernatural. Ann Putnam, age 11, was declared to be showing similar signs of the supernatural. On February 29, under extreme pressure from magistrates Jonathan Corwin and John Hathorne, the girls blamed, with absolute conviction, three women for their affliction: Sarah Good, a homeless vagrant; Sarah Osborne, an elderly and impoverished woman, and Tituba, the Caribbean slave of the Parris'.

Claiming to be possessed by the devil, the accusation of the local women was of witchcraft. So began a sequence of events that would quickly spiral out of control, mass hysteria ensued with accusations mounting on a seemingly unstoppable tide that would lead to some, even to this day believing that there must have been truth among the stories.

Such was the severity of the situation that, by the order of Governor William Phipps, a special court was convened to put the growing number of accused on trial. The first case brought before the special court was that of Bridget Bishop, an older woman known for her gossipy ways and untethered promiscuity. When asked if she committed witchcraft, Bishop responded, "I am as innocent as the child unborn." The defence must not have been compelling for she was found guilty and, on June 10, became the first person to be hung on what later would be known as the now infamous Gallows Hill.

Immediately following the execution of Bridget Bishop, the court adjourned for 20 days while it sought advice from New England's most influential ministers "upon the state of things as they then stood". Their collective response was dated June 15 and composed by Cotton Mather as follows:

> *The return of several ministers consulted by his excellency and the honorable council upon the present witchcraft in Salem village.*

1. The afflicted state of our poor neighbours, that are now suffering by molestations from the invisible world, we apprehend so deplorable, that we think their condition calls for the utmost help of all persons in their several capacities.

2. We cannot but, with all thankfulness, acknowledge the success which the merciful God has given unto the sedulous and assiduous endeavours of our honourable rulers, to detect the abominable witchcrafts which have been committed in the country, humbly praying, that the discovery of those mysterious and mischievous wickednesses may be perfected.

3. We judge that, in the prosecution of these and all such witchcrafts, there is need of a very critical and exquisite caution, lest by too much credulity for things received only upon the Devil's authority, there be a door opened for a long train of miserable consequences, and Satan get an advantage over us; for we should not be ignorant of his devices.

4. As in complaints upon witchcrafts, there may be matters of inquiry which do not amount unto matters of presumption, and there may be matters of presumption which yet may not be matters of conviction, so it is necessary, that all proceedings thereabout be managed with an exceeding tenderness towards those that may be complained of, especially if they have been persons formerly of an unblemished reputation.

5. When the first inquiry is made into the circumstances of such as may lie under the just suspicion of witchcrafts, we could wish that there may be admitted as little as is possible of such noise, company and openness as may too hastily expose them that are examined, and that there may no thing be used as a test for the trial of the suspected, the lawfulness whereof may be doubted among the people of God; but that the directions given by such judicious writers as Perkins and Bernard [be consulted in such a case].

6. Presumptions whereupon persons may be committed, and, much more, convictions whereupon persons may be condemned as guilty of witchcrafts, ought certainly to be more considerable than barely the accused person's being represented by a specter unto the afflicted; inasmuch as it is an undoubted and notorious thing, that a demon may, by God's permission, appear, even to ill purposes, in the shape of an innocent, yea, and a virtuous man. Nor can we esteem alterations made in the sufferers, by a look or touch of the accused, to be an infallible evidence of guilt, but frequently liable to be abused by the Devil's legerdemains.

7. We know not whether some remarkable affronts given to the Devils by our disbelieving those testimonies whose whole force and strength is from them alone, may not put a period unto the progress of the dreadful calamity begun upon us, in the accusations of so many persons, whereof some, we hope, are yet clear from the great transgression laid unto their charge.

8. Nevertheless, we cannot but humbly recommend unto the government, the speedy and vigorous prosecution of such as have rendered themselves obnoxious, according to the direction given in the laws of God, and the wholesome statutes of the English nation, for the detection of witchcrafts.

Over the course of the months that followed nineteen people were sentenced to death by hanging, one was pressed to death and over a hundred men, women and children were also accused. Several more of the accused died in prison.

When the momentum began to wane and public perception of the trials started to alter, the convictions were later annulled and the families of those executed were granted indemnities.

Despite the fact that these were not the first people executed for witchcraft and that Salem was not the only area embroiled in the events of 1692; the Salem Witch Trials gathered increased profile for the scale of the convictions and spread of the hysteria.

To this day the good folk of Salem have the deeds of their towns past indelibly inked into the pages of its history. That history leads us to wonder at the spell that could possibly have been woven to take hold of a community of the sane to make it behave with the actions of the insane.

The following are the names of those who were sentenced to death and executed during the Salem Witch Trials

Bridget Bishop

Hanged - June 10, 1692

Rebecca (Towne) Nurse

Hanged - July 19, 1692

Sarah (Solart) Good

Hanged - July 19, 1692

Elizabeth (Jackson) Howe

Hanged - July 19, 1692

Sarah (Averill) Wildes

Hanged - July 19, 1692

Susannah (North) Martin

Hanged - July 19, 1692

George Burroughs

Hanged - August 19, 1692

Martha (Allen) Carrier

Hanged - August 19, 1692

George Jacobs, Sr.

Hanged - August 19, 1692

John Proctor

Hanged - August 19, 1692

John Willard

Hanged - August 19, 1692

Giles Corey

Pressed to death September 19, 1692

Martha Corey

Hanged - September 22, 1692

Mary (Towne) Eastey

Hanged - September 22, 1692

Alice Parker

Hanged - September 22, 1692

Mary (Ayer) Parker

Hanged - September 22, 1692

Ann Pudeator

Hanged - September 22, 1692

Margaret (Stevenson) Scott

Hanged - September 22, 1692

Wilmot Redd

Hanged - September 22, 1692

Samuel Wardwell Sr.

Hanged - September 22, 1692

RIP

Printed in Great Britain
by Amazon.co.uk, Ltd.,
Marston Gate.